THE MIDNIGHT GROCER

Brian Beresford

ISBN: 978-1-914933-21-9

A copy of this book is deposited with the British Library

Published By: -

i2i

PUBLISHING

i2i Publishing. Manchester.
www.i2ipublishing.co.uk

Remembering Bruce Cross
Teacher, storyteller, friend

Contents

Have you ever heard a sound that you love more than any other, one that gives you so much pleasure that you call it your 'golden sound' and want to try to make it yourself?

Imagine how it would feel if an even better version of your 'golden sound' woke you up in the middle of the night. Wouldn't you want to know what or who had made that sound?

And what if you were passing by the end of a street that you had been warned to keep well away from when you heard a very different sound – the cry of a child who needed help – would you dare to investigate?...

1. The Golden Sound

It was always the same on the last day of the school year. The children were tired, the teachers were tired, the classrooms looked tired and even the weather seemed to be tired. After a sunny summer term, in baking hot classrooms with no air conditioning, it was time for what a lot of people call the summer holidays. Chaaya was aware that many of her friends would be going away to sandy beaches, swimming pools and weeks of fun, but for her it meant that time would be spent in and around home as usual.

At the very end of the day, Chaaya and the rest of her Year 4 class gave three loud cheers for their teacher. Miss Robinson's table was virtually hidden by presents from her adoring pupils, and Chaaya felt sad that she hadn't given anything herself. Chaaya waited until all the other children had left the room, and then slowly approached Miss Robinson.

"I made you a card, Miss Robinson. It's only a little one though." Chaaya felt strangely self-conscious as she passed a folded piece of paper to her favourite teacher and shyly turned away as it was opened.

"Oh, Chaaya, it's lovely," said Miss Robinson, and she meant it. Chaaya's picture of a woman lying on a beach and the message, 'Thank you for being my best teacher ever', would take pride of place in her heart as well as on her window ledge. Of course, she knew Chaaya very well after teaching such a delightful, hard-working, and caring girl for a year, and understood the financial difficulties faced by the Williams family. Chaaya's mum worked seven days a week as an office and household cleaner in order to pay for the food, clothes and other basic needs for Chaaya, her ten-year-old brother Jaden, and herself.

Chaaya quietly made her way to the door and, as she turned to look back at the classroom she was leaving, both she and Miss Robinson could see tears in the other's eyes. They waved, both knowing that they had meant a great deal to each other.

Every day after school, Chaaya made her way home with her best friend and next-door neighbour,

Amber. Although two years older than her, Amber had always been Chaaya's closest friend. Chaaya's mum, Dayana and Amber's mum, Laura, seemed to live in each other's houses almost as much as their own and the girls used to pretend that they all lived together.

Chaaya's mum usually arrived home from work at about five o'clock, and between the end of school and then the two girls made their own fun. On Fridays they always went to the park, where Jaden and his friends played their weekly many-a-side football game.

Jaden was known in the district as a talented footballer. Tall, athletic, and blessed with two good feet, he was the school's top scorer, even though he was a year younger than all the others in the team. When the weekly Friday kickabout took place, everyone wanted him to be on their side.

The two girls knew not to get too close to the football action and took their usual seats on the swings behind one of the goals. Jaden had once warned his sister not to react when he scored a goal or if he missed the target, saying, "You cramp my style", but he secretly loved the fact that she wanted to watch him.

Chaaya was aware that Miss Robinson lived in a house straight across the road from the park entrance, and she used to look out for her favourite teacher arriving home. Sure enough, Chaaya was lucky enough to see her carrying lots of boxes and bags into her house today and was very pleased when Miss Robinson gave her a cheery wave. Of course, Chaaya waved back and told Amber, "She's the best teacher in the world."

"Is she? I always thought Mr Griffiths was the best, at least that's what he kept telling us. But I have to admit that your Miss Robinson has lovely long golden hair and Mr Griffiths is as bald as a baby's bum. He's kind and good at telling jokes, though. So why do you think Miss Robinson is better?"

Chaaya could think of lots of reasons but decided to tell Amber that Miss Robinson always seemed to know if somebody needed her. "She says she has eyes in the back of her head, that's why she's the best." They both laughed and turned their attention to the football.

Chaaya had been watching from her swing for just a few moments when she saw Jaden swerve with perfect balance past two defenders and chip the ball expertly over the advancing goalkeeper for a wonderful goal. She cheered silently inside her own body and pretended not to notice. She would congratulate her brother later when they were watching TV that evening.

It wasn't only her pride in Jaden's skill and sportsmanship that drew Chaaya to watch the football. She loved to hear the sound of the football being kicked and the *WHOOSH* it made as it flew through the air. That *WHOOSH* was simply her favourite sound and, a few minutes after Jaden scored, she decided to tell Amber about it.

"Amber, what's your golden sound?"

"What's a golden sound when it's at home?"

"You know, a sound that's so good you can't get enough of it."

"I have no idea what you're talking about."

"Well okay, I'll tell you what mine is then. It's the sound a football makes when it's kicked really hard."

"You're silly." Amber often said "you're silly" when she didn't want to talk about something, but Chaaya didn't mind. The sound of the football was her golden sound and that was it. If Amber didn't have a golden sound, that was just fine.

As usual, Chaaya and Amber walked home together. Chaaya always made sure she got back a few minutes before Jaden who didn't like his friends to see the two of them walking together. Amber's parents both worked shifts in a car factory and at least one of them was usually at home to keep an eye on them all.

"I can't come out after tea tonight," said Amber. "Dad's taking me swimming, so I'll see you tomorrow."

Amber mentioned her dad a lot. The Hodgson family seemed to do many exciting things together, and Chaaya was happy that her friend had a kind dad. Although Chaaya didn't have a dad, she knew that she was lucky to have such a great mum and brother.

"Hi Mum, I'm home!" Chaaya rushed through the house to the kitchen and gave her a big hug.

"What have I done to deserve star treatment?" Dayana Williams giggled in a way that only her children ever heard.

"I didn't want to leave Miss Robinson's class, Mum, but I think she liked being my teacher."

"Let me tell you a fact, young lady - Miss Robinson loved being your teacher. I know that because she told me so. Your next teacher will say the same thing too." Before Chaaya could respond, the sound of big brother arriving at high speed hit their ear drums. "Hey, Jaden, are you sad about the end of term too?"

"No way! And the big news is that I scored eight goals and we won 9-1. The second goal was the best, though; I dribbled past their entire defence and hit an unstoppable shot past Big Harry."

"*WHOOSH*," shouted Chaaya.

2. The Thing

Chaaya slept well that night and, in her dream, she played football at Wembley Stadium. Jaden was running through a packed defence before sending a perfect pass through to her. After controlling the ball and looking up at the goal, she prepared to shoot…

WHOOOOOOSH - Chaaya woke suddenly. What was that noise? It wasn't particularly loud, but it seemed to come from just outside her bedroom window, and it reminded her of the 'golden sound' of the ball being kicked hard, but this kick must have been much harder, and the ball must have travelled faster and for much longer than ever before. Still half asleep, Chaaya checked the time. It was midnight, so it must have been part of her dream after all, and her dream goal must have been the greatest ever! Chaaya smiled and chuckled to herself as sleepiness returned.

Dayana was ready to leave for work by 8.25 am. She hated the weekends. It would be great to be able to spend a whole weekend with the children just for once, but offices don't clean themselves and most of the hard work had to be carried out by teams of weekend cleaners putting in extra hours.

"Don't forget to let Laura know what you are doing today."

"Yes Mum," chorused Jaden and Chaaya. Laura would be looking after them as if they were her own daughter, Amber. In return for weekend childcare, Dayana was happy to clean, wash and iron for Laura, and both families understood and respected each other for being the great friends they were rather than co-workers.

Jaden waited until his mum set off walking to work before leaving Chaaya in no doubt about his Saturday plans. "Big Harry is organising a massive tournament for us all today. It starts at ten, so I'd best be off soon. Can you tell Laura for me?"

"Of course I will. I might come down to watch later." She hesitated before asking the question that had been bottled up inside her all morning. "Can I join in for a bit?"

"Join in with what?"

"With the game."

"Don't be daft."

"Why not?"

Jaden knew he had to be careful how he answered this one. "Cos the others wouldn't let you, that's why."

"Aw, that's not fair." Sadly, Chaaya knew that was the end of the discussion and, saying no more, she switched on the television.

Remembering to take his phone so he could always contact Laura if he needed to, Jaden had been long gone when Amber knocked on the back door.

"Why are you knocking? Just come straight in like you always do," called Chaaya.

"I can't get past this thing," shouted Amber. Chaaya opened the back door and saw Amber standing on top of an enormous... well, an enormous... thing! Amber asked the obvious question. "What's this... this... thing doing here?"

The 'thing' appeared to be a huge yellowish-silver shiny metallic box of some sort. That shine reminded Chaaya of the bodywork of a luxurious car.

It was over a metre high, and almost entirely filled the back yard, which was about three metres long on each side.

Chaaya jumped up onto it; it felt solid and hard under her feet.

"How did they get it here?" asked Amber. Each terraced house in the street had a tiny back yard which could only be reached by walking up 'the backs', a narrow alley no wider than a small car, and each yard had a small gate in its high wall.

"I have no idea what it is or who brought it," replied Chaaya.

"Your mum must have ordered it."

"I guess so, but she never said anything to me."

"Do you think there's anything in it?"

"How would I know?" Chaaya looked all over what she could see of the object for any way of opening it; there didn't appear to be one.

"I know what it is," said Amber.

"Go on then, what is it?"

"It's one of those prisons nobody can escape from. I reckon there'll be a dangerous criminal inside," she joked. "Let's leave it here and go out. I'll go round to the front door."

Chaaya wasn't sure if she ought to phone her mum at work but decided the object would still be there when she arrived home. Dayana would know something about it, and she could explain it to them later. Chaaya went back into the house, locking the back door just as Amber arrived at the front. "Let's be off. I've told Mum we're going for a walk and will be back at one o'clock, and I've got my phone."

"There's somewhere I want to go," replied Chaaya, "and something I want to try."

"What's that?"

"I'll tell you later."

"It's not something to do with your stupid golden sound, is it?"

"It might be." Chaaya didn't want Amber to think she was obsessed with the notion of a golden sound, but she really wanted to know if the sound she had heard in the middle of the night was real, and if it could be made by kicking a ball as hard as possible.

"You're silly."

As Chaaya slammed the front door so that it locked, she was so busy thinking of how she could find a way of kicking a ball as hard as possible that she didn't notice that, just behind the inside of the front door, there was a small thin packet, no more than ten centimetres long, wrapped in a yellowish-silver material.

3. The Big Match

When Chaaya and Amber arrived at the park later that morning the footballers were still there. A tournament was taking place: Big Harry had organised all the boys into six teams of five or six, which gave everyone the same amount of time to play and time to sit around between games, eyeing up the opposition. Jaden was absent-mindedly chewing a bit of grass and had just started chatting with his teammates when he spotted that the girls were coming closer. He hoped that Chaaya wouldn't embarrass him by asking if she could join in.

"Race to the swings?" Amber always seemed to be ready to run.

"Okay," confirmed Chaaya, and without further hesitation she shouted, "Ready, go!"

The girls couldn't have been more evenly matched, but today they stopped short of the swings, having noticed that someone they didn't recognise was sitting on one of them.

The other girl turned to face them and smiled. "Hello, I'm Sally."

After a quick exchange of introductions, Sally suddenly said, "I have to go now." She turned and ran and, as she did so, Chaaya said, "Sally has the longest ginger hair I have ever seen."

"You mean auburn, not ginger."

"Or maybe it's strawberry blonde?" Chaaya liked that description of the colour best, but Amber was more interested in something else she had noticed about Sally and added, "Yeah, but look at her run, we could both easily beat her any day."

Jaden and his team, which they had named Blasters, were ready for the final match of the tournament. Blasters were unbeaten and so were their opponents, City Blues. Jaden gathered his team around him in a huddle, the way professional captains do before kick-off.

"Right, this is what we have to do... we play a non-stop attacking game... shoot on sight... don't let 'em settle... work non-stop... never give in... ready? 3,2,1... BLASTERS!"

"BLASTERS!" they all shouted in reply and ran to their positions.

Blasters went into attacking mode straight from the kick-off. City Blues struggled to cope with their pace and skill and the entire team immediately dropped back towards their own goal, forming a packed defence.

Five minutes passed and there was no score. Blasters were sending lots of crosses and shots into the City Blues' goalmouth, but they were all either hitting Blues players or going wide. This pattern of play continued until half time, when both sets of players sat down with their teammates and had a well-earned break.

Jaden was the first to stand up. "We have to try something different," he said. "Instead of passing every time I think we should just try to dribble straight through 'em."

"How do we do that against this lot?" asked Kim, and the others moaned that they would never score, no matter how hard they tried.

Jaden wanted to show his teammates that a positive attitude was needed and, grabbing the ball, he stood up and ran with it to the centre spot. He certainly sounded up for the challenge. "Right, let's get on with it." The other members of Blasters leapt up and ran to their starting positions. City Blues looked determined, they clearly meant business, and the game resumed at a high tempo.

Two of the team's other players, Kim and Luke, both tried to do what Jaden had suggested, and they each ran hard at their opponents with the ball at their feet, but both failed because they simply couldn't find a way past the City Blues' tough players.

Jaden decided it was time for him to let his own skill shine through. With the ball under his control, he turned and headed back halfway to his own goal.

Blasters' goalkeeper Rayan was shocked to see one of his own teammates bearing down on his goal and he yelled, "What are you doing, you maniac?" But Jaden stopped, put his foot on the ball, winked at Rayan and spun round. Just as he had expected, half the City Blues team had followed him, seeing what they thought might be their only chance to score, but Jaden now ran towards them, dribbling first past one, then two, then three, before reaching shooting distance from the Blues' goal. The final defender was the solidly reliable Baz, whose 'they shall not pass' attitude was known far and wide. To those watching and to all the others playing, what followed seemed to happen in slow motion. Jaden put his foot on the ball once again, before dropping his left shoulder and spinning to his right, the ball at his feet. But Baz had seen such tricks before and his strong frame moved like lightning, taking him feet-first straight onto Jaden's right knee with such force that the scream seemed louder than any other sound ever made in a football match.

The watching tournament organiser Big Harry immediately leapt to his feet and shouted, "Penalty!" He sprinted onto the pitch, picked up the ball and put it onto the penalty spot. All the players from both teams had run towards where the incident took place.

Jaden was lying on the floor, holding his knee, and trying not to cry. Baz, who everyone knew was sometimes rather too heavy in the tackle, was kneeling and saying, "Sorry mate" repeatedly. Some of the Blasters team looked ready to fight any City Blues players who so much as looked at them.

A moment later Jaden looked up at Baz's concerned face, stood up and held out his hand in friendship, saying, "It's okay mate, I'm fine."

"I didn't mean to take you out, Jaden, honestly."

"I know, but it's still a penalty, isn't it?" reminded Jaden and he turned to look for the ball; the penalty kick would be his big chance to score. But to his horror he suddenly realised that his little sister was about to ruin everything!

Chaaya had heard Big Harry shout, "Penalty!" and saw him carry the ball to the spot, leaving it there unattended while the players surrounded her injured brother. Without realising the implications of what she was doing, she ran onto the pitch and stopped three metres from the ball. The empty goal was at Chaaya's mercy. Here was her big chance, not merely to take a penalty, nor to become accepted as a footballer in her own right, but to kick that ball as hard as it could possibly be kicked and then to just listen.

The other footballers now saw what Jaden was looking at and they froze. Something about Chaaya's expression told them not to interfere. After the deepest of deep breaths Chaaya positively charged at the ball. The power of her kick was impressive, even by Baz's standards. The ball flew through the empty goal and way beyond, passing the swings where Amber still sat, open-mouthed, and it finally came to rest in the hedge after travelling a total distance of about 50 metres.

The reaction of the players was unusual and extraordinary. Some cheered, a few clapped, there were shouts of, "Great goal!" and others simply looked astonished at the power they had just seen unleashed. But Jaden was the first to reach Chaaya.

"Okay, so what did you do that for?"

Chaaya knew her brother wouldn't understand but decided to tell him the truth. "I just wanted to hear the best '*whoosh*' I had ever heard."

"So, did you?"

"No. It wasn't anywhere near as good as the one I heard at midnight." With that Chaaya walked slowly back towards Amber, seemingly in a kind of trance.

Jaden had no idea what his sister meant, but he knew what he must do next. Despite the searing pain in his knee, he ran to the hedge, brought the ball back to the penalty spot and prepared to take the kick that would win the tournament for Blasters.

4. Weekly Shopping

Chaaya and Amber had been having a great day until it started to rain in the afternoon, and by the time they got back to their street they were both soaked from head to toe. Just as they arrived at the front of their houses, Dayana, running from the opposite direction, met them with a cheery, "Hi, you two. Who's the wettest girl in town? And don't bother trying to answer - let's get in and get dry."

"See you tomorrow, Chaaya," said Amber as her front door slammed behind her as if it wanted to help to keep the rain out of the house.

Dayana turned the key to her own front door and was the first to notice something unusual, a small yellowish-silver packet that appeared to have come through the letter box. She picked it up. "Well, Chaaya, it's not my birthday, not yours and not Jaden's but somebody must love us."

Chaaya suddenly had a strange feeling, guessing that the packet must have something to do with the same coloured 'thing' in the back yard.

"Mum, you need to know that somebody else must have been here this morning before we went out."

"What? Who?" Dayana wondered if her daughter was about to tell her that a burglar had been trying to get in, and her mind started to race.

Chaaya answered quickly, before her mum could become too anxious. Calling, "Follow me," she ran through the front room, into the kitchen and out to the yard. She still wondered if the 'thing' had really been there in the morning, but now she knew for certain that it was real. "There!"

Dayana stood, staring in disbelief at the huge object in front of them. Gasping with surprise, she dropped the packet onto the floor. Chaaya calmly picked it up and said, "This might have something to do with it, Mum. It's the same colour."

Dayana continued to stare at the huge object. "I… I… have… no... idea… what this is!"

"Should I open this packet thing?"

"I think I should do that." Dayana was worried that something awful might happen to Chaaya and decided that she must take some motherly responsibility. After all, this object might contain chemicals, maybe even explosives or something unthinkable.

Chaaya handed the packet to her mum who found that, despite feeling as if it were made from a strong kind of material, it was simple to tear open. Dayana looked timidly inside before lifting out a short, thin yellowish-silver object with her finger and thumb. "It looks a bit like a short pencil, and it feels really smooth and a bit warm."

"Warm?" asked Chaaya, "How can it be warm? Can I touch it, Mum?"

As soon as Chaaya touched the thin object she knew exactly what her mum meant; "Wow, it feels somehow like magic, a warm magic wand," and, without realising what she was doing, Chaaya waved the magic pencil wand in the air.

What happened next was even more magical - in fact it was the most magical thing you could ever imagine. The huge object that had almost entirely filled the back yard just vanished; one moment it was there and the next, just as Chaaya waved the magic pencil wand, it completely disappeared.

Dayana and Chaaya both screamed and ran back into the kitchen and hugged each other tightly. It seemed like forever before they could get their breath back, but when they finally spoke, they seemed to have lost all sense of reality. "What?" "Why?" "It's so weird," "I don't understand," and "How?" were just some of the things that were spluttering from their mouths and some other words that they would not normally say were mixed in with them too.

Chaaya suddenly realised that the magic pencil wand also seemed to have disappeared. Dayana, trying to speak calmly, managed to croak, "I'm never going out there again," and at the time she meant it, but Chaaya was already opening the back door. With eyes half closed, as if she were expecting to see something terrible, she took a step forward. The back yard looked exactly as it was supposed to, apart from the newly appeared pile of food!

"Mum, did you leave the shopping out here?"

"I haven't been for the shopping yet. I'm going later tonight. Why?"

"Because it's already here."

"It can't be!" Then Dayana remembered that the unbelievable now seemed to be happening quite regularly, and she bravely joined Chaaya in the yard. Together they picked up the packets, cans, bags, jars, fresh fruit and vegetables, cartons and all the other items they normally bought from the supermarket, plus the lovely addition of two chocolate orange treats.

Jaden didn't play football every minute of the day; that would have been impossible even for someone as obsessed as he was, but he had a great time with his friends. All young people know that there's nothing better than being with others your own age, just 'hanging out', and it was a tired but happy group of four, Jaden, Big Harry, Luke and Kim, that wandered slowly towards the row of houses where they all lived. Jaden's knee was hurting, and it had bled a bit, but he saw it as some sort of badge of courage that could only be worn by a goalscoring hero like himself.

Just around the corner from where Jaden lived there was a narrow alley which was the way through to the back yards of the houses in Paradise Street. Despite its name, Paradise Street had a reputation throughout the town as somewhere to be avoided. All the children knew that half the houses were empty and that some were boarded up. Big Harry had told the others that his dad said there were criminals hiding out in some of the houses, and everyone knew that homeless people and even drug users were in there somewhere.

Heavy rain was falling by the time the four boys reached the alleyway. Big Harry, Luke and Kim ran ahead of Jaden, whose leg was slowing him down far more than he would have liked. As Jaden passed the end of Paradise Street, he could just hear something or someone making a strange high-pitched sound. He stopped in his tracks and listened: there it was again. At first, he thought it could be a cat, or maybe a crow, but then he wondered if it could be the cry of a person in trouble.

"Hey lads, come here!" The others stopped and looked at their friend.

"What's up?" asked Kim.

"I'm not going to carry you, if that's what you want," shouted Big Harry. But they could see that Jaden needed them for some reason and they ran back to where he stood, listening.

"Can you hear it?"

"Hear what?" the others asked in unison, which made them giggle.

"Shut up and listen! Somebody's crying."

"I'll be crying if I don't get home soon," insisted Luke, "I'm soaking wet."

Big Harry, who everyone looked up to as a leader, didn't seem interested. "Come on, let's be off. What happens in Paradise Street is none of our business." He was echoing words his dad had used and that made him seem so grown up, he thought.

"Yeah, let's get away from here," agreed Kim, and the three uninjured ones shot off in the direction of their own homes.

"Thanks for your help," shouted Jaden sarcastically. The high-pitched sound continued, and Jaden knew that, despite what he had been told, he was about to enter the alley that led to Paradise Street. He felt sure that someone needed help, that someone was in distress.

As he approached the back of the second house Jaden realised that the sound was coming from its yard. Slowly and carefully, he peeped through the gap in the back wall. A girl with long auburn hair was sitting on the wet ground next to a pile of cardboard boxes, crying loudly. "What's wrong with you?" Jaden asked anxiously.

The girl looked up, startled. "Go away!" she yelled and stuck her tongue out.

It was obvious that the girl was in distress. She was filthy, with black fingernails and mud on her clothes and face. "You should be indoors," said Jaden quietly, trying to stay calm.

"I don't live here anyway."

"Then why are you here?"

"Where else can I go?"

"Why don't you go home?"

"I can't, I just can't, and I'm so hungry." The girl still hadn't stopped crying. It seemed to Jaden that she could have been crying for hours.

Jaden had reached the point where he knew he must do something. The girl reminded him of his sister in some ways; she appeared to be about the same age and height, and he wished that Chaaya were there too. Perhaps, if he got home quickly, he could persuade Chaaya to come back with him. "You stay here - I'll be back soon," he said reassuringly, and despite the pain in his leg, he ran home as quickly as he could.

Jaden flew through the front door and into the kitchen. Dayana was sorting through all the parts of their mysterious gift, and Chaaya was holding two chocolate oranges.

"Oh great, you've been for the groceries already." Jaden's eyes flashed round the room, eyeing the collection of provision, and Chaaya laughed.

"Look, Mr Hungry, we've each got a special treat," she said, and gave him one of the chocolate oranges. "You'll never guess what's happened..."

But Jaden didn't wait to hear any more. He took the chocolate orange and ran out through the front door without closing it. "Someone's in a rush." Dayana assumed that he was going to have finished all the chocolate segments even before he reached the end of the street.

She was wrong, of course. Jaden had just one thought in his head, and for once it had nothing to do with football. He almost tripped over a mangy old tom cat that was lapping water out of a puddle in the entrance to the Paradise Street alleyway and was back with the girl far quicker than even he could have imagined. She was still sobbing but looked up in surprise when she saw Jaden who was holding out his hand with something lovely for her. "You won't be hungry for much longer."

"Is that for… for me?"

"Yeah, it's all yours. Don't offer me any, 'cos I won't take it."

It came as no surprise to Jaden that the girl opened the shiny wrapper and took out one segment, then another, and another and so on, shoving each one after the others into her ever-filling mouth. Jaden had never seen anyone eat so quickly; even Big Harry, who was the official school sponge cake eating champion, would have struggled to keep up with her. The whole chocolate orange disappeared from sight in front of them and, after a big burp, the girl smiled, her muddy and chocolate-streaked face making her look quite clown-like.

"You rescued me," she said, and Jaden suddenly felt as if he could have been one of King Arthur's knights in a former life. She stood up. "Now I have to go."

Jaden was surprised that she didn't say more, and if he hadn't thought it would make him sound like someone from a sloppy romantic film, he would have asked, "Do you really have to?" Instead, he just muttered, "I hope you'll be okay."

The girl's voice was strong now, and although she didn't actually thank Jaden, her two words, "I'm fine," told him what he wanted to hear. She started to leave him, and as she turned to run into the depths of Paradise Street, he heard her final message to him. "I'm Sally!"

Jaden could run no further. His leg hurt, he was tired and very hungry. Hobbling home, he would never have guessed that he was going to be told to sit down and listen carefully as two excited family members described the strange happenings that had taken place that day.

5. The Mission

When Sally reached the far end of Paradise Street, she decided it was time for her to rest and think about her adventure on this special day for her. It was special because Friday 23rd July had been her first day on Earth, the day her mission had begun, and she concentrated very hard in order to be able to enter her personal caravan, the between-worlds room that had been created just for her, a place where she had everything she needed for the coming days. Throwing off her auburn wig, Sally sat down with Claude, her long haired brown and white guinea pig, and gave him the cuddle he so desired.

Planet 3 was virtually the same as Earth in most ways, except that the scientists who lived and worked there had discovered ways of travelling to their sister world, Earth, whereas Earth humans had absolutely no idea that Planet 3 existed.

Sally's 'mission' was what Earth school children might refer to as a holiday project. Her teacher, Professor Xander, had been delighted when he received Sally's outline plan for her mission, and he had persuaded the school director to award a grant of 10,500 sperglons to cover all the costs. The mission had taken months to plan, and Sally had been carefully briefed on just exactly what she could and could not do.

Sally's final briefing had taken place two days before her adventure had begun. Her pre-mission appointment with Professor Xander had gone smoothly, although she wished that he hadn't taken so long going through details that Sally had already memorised.

"Your choice of mission is excellent, Sally. You are to spend up to eighteen days on Earth, getting to know the Williams family of 24 Rankin Street in order to assess whether or not they, being representative of Earth humans, are capable of selfless acts that can improve the wellbeing of others. The reason for your mission is clear: Planet 3 humans have observed countless examples of the selfishness of Earth humans, who over many centuries have made enemies of their own kind, fought wars, created discrimination between people and continued to cause great harm to their own planet through enormous and potentially irreversible damage to their own environment. Am I clearly expressing your aims, Sally?"

Sally admired Xander's straightforward bluntness. "Yes, Professor, and of course the implications of Earth human behaviours are huge for us. Planet 3 dwellers are now beginning to suffer the consequences of the Earth humans' actions. Planet 3 and Earth must exist side by side in mutual harmony if both are to survive. If Earth were to become a wasteland Planet 3 would eventually follow because, since we discovered that Earth really exists, many of our species have been there and the harmful influences that have been brought back here have spread alarmingly quickly."

"Well said, Sally! Your mission might be tiny in the whole scheme of things, but it is only by understanding how Earth humans relate to each other that we can evaluate their chances of having a future of any kind. Now let's get down to the practicalities of your mission. As you know, we have been awarded 10,500 sperglons in order that you can carry out your work, but remember that you must be careful not to spend more than that total. If your work costs just one sperglon more your parents will have to pay the additional amount, and we both know that Mr and Mrs Kwolek have already expressed their fears that they would not be able to meet that demand." Xander was being clear about the financial implications of the mission, but Sally felt certain that she wouldn't overspend. The money was all held by her school, and she could only exceed the total if she were to use Earth money for any reason.

"Thank you, Professor. My parents are very grateful that you have obtained so much finance for my mission."

"And now Sally, I have to ask you a few questions, partly to check that you are clear about the detail of the mission, and also to give you the chance to ask me anything at this stage. Firstly, how will you get to Earth and where will you live?"

"I will concentrate very hard on my personal caravan and that should be enough to get me into it whenever and wherever I need it."

"Correct. You have proved that you are able to enter the caravan with one hundred percent success in your training. Sally, what else will be in your personal caravan?"

"All I need to live happily until the end date of Monday 9th August, including all my food, clothes, books, television, computer, kitchen appliances, a fully equipped bathroom and bedroom and an endless supply of water. Oh, and lots of photographs of my family, of course. The personal caravan also allows me to observe the Earth humans even when I am not in direct contact with them because it has been fitted with the new Orconiwave viewer, linked into my senses and memory."

"You have chosen to take an animal with you, I believe."

Sally's face lit up. "Yes, Claude, my guinea pig. All his hay, pellets, clean bedding and adventure playground equipment will be there for him too. The

Eco-tech fresh vegetable system will ensure he has good fresh nibbles."

"What else have you asked us to provide in order that you can fulfil your mission?" Xander knew the answer to this question, of course, and he was very proud that Sally had been so ingenious in devising this aspect of her mission.

"You will send a yellow silvercrate to the back yard of 24 Rankin Street on three successive Fridays at midnight. The silvercrates will contain the items I have listed after previously using the Orconiwave viewer to observe the shopping habits of Mrs Williams."

"Excellent, Sally! That seems to cover the most important details. Is there anything you want to ask me?"

"Just one thing, Professor - am I allowed to make friends with Earth humans? I don't want to be lonely."

"Of course, Sally. The whole point of you being there is that you should get to know people well enough to be able to reach meaningful conclusions.

At the moment, we can observe Earth humans from a distance, but we cannot tell what they are thinking. Close contact with the Williams family and others will give you greater understanding of their thoughts and behaviour. Don't forget that you can be an actor; you have to play the part of an Earth human in order to be accepted without question. And, of course, you must wear your special wig. We don't want anyone to find out that you have eyes in the back of your head!"

"Is that the only difference between us and Earth humans?"

"The only physical difference, yes, so do not forget to wear it!" Xander stood up and showed Sally to the door. "The rest, Sally, is up to you. We will be observing you even though you won't be able to see us, so don't worry. Enjoy your mission, but just don't overspend the sperglons."

Sally laughed. "I won't." And with that she ran home to spend the next two days with her parents before the time came to enter her personal caravan.

6. A Family Decision

It was understandable that Jaden thought Chaaya and Dayana had made up the story about the way their groceries had arrived. How could anyone with even a tiny bit of common sense believe anything about an appearing and disappearing yellowish-silver metallic box and a delivery of weekly shopping that seemed to have come from fairies?

A few days had passed since the food had been deposited in the back yard and the family had stopped talking about the strange sequence of events, but of course they spent a lot of time thinking about it.

Chaaya knew for certain that what she experienced had been real and wondered how Amber remembered the moment when she first saw the object. Of course, Amber hadn't been there when the magic pencil wand made the food appear, and she hadn't mentioned it since. After all, she had seen the huge object in the back yard and probably thought it was just something ordinary but unusual, maybe something that was of no interest to her and none of her business.

Dayana was in no doubt that something incredible had happened. She didn't believe in supernatural events and understood that magicians are really very clever performers who sometimes use science as part of their acts, harmlessly tricking people for entertainment purposes. She wondered if she might have witnessed a miracle but couldn't possibly understand why that should happen to them. Despite her puzzlement, she was grateful that her weekly shopping had somehow been provided for her, and she was satisfied that the food was of the highest quality. The apples and pears were perfectly fresh, as if they had been newly picked from trees, something Dayana couldn't always say about fruit from her usual supermarket.

Jaden couldn't stop thinking about the girl he had tried to help. He said nothing to his family about what he had done for a few reasons. He didn't want his mum to find out that he had ventured into Paradise Street - Dayana would be angry if she knew he had gone there despite being warned many times that "dangerous people" who could hurt him might be there. He didn't know how to rationalise his feelings about the girl, but he recognised that as soon as he had heard and seen her crying, he had to do something to try and help her. She had desperately needed something to eat, and he was worried that she might be in that terrible position again at any time. Could there be others who could help? Jaden wished he knew. But he was also anxious about something else - if the other boys knew what he had done would they make fun of him for being 'soft'? Jaden felt that he should keep quiet about Sally. The girl was real, but he didn't feel like sharing her reality with anyone else.

That evening, while the family were sitting in their kitchen finishing off the last of the juicy apples they had received in their surprise gift, Dayana decided it was time to raise the subject of the weekend's events. "Have either of you told anyone else about what happened last Saturday?"

Jaden's reply was almost instant. "Do you mean when I scored with that brilliant chip over the keeper?"

Chaaya accepted that Jaden still didn't believe they were telling the truth about the strange event and answered her mum sensibly. "I haven't told anyone else, but Amber was the first one to see the big object that filled our back yard, so she knows about it."

"Do you think she will have told any others?" asked Dayana.

"I don't think so, but she certainly would have done if she had seen it disappear."

"Well then, I don't think we have anything to worry about."

"Such as what?" interrupted Jaden.

Dayana took a deep breath. "Such as the press. If it got onto social media, we would be besieged by photographers and reporters."

Jaden continued, "Then the whole world would know you were nuts. We might even have to dress up as fairies and pixies for them! I would have to pretend that I don't know you." They all laughed.

"So it's decided then," concluded Dayana. "We keep it to ourselves - okay?"

"Okay!" the children replied together.

7. A Special Teacher

Chaaya couldn't believe they had been on summer holiday for a week already, but that reality was underlined when Amber's face appeared at the front window.

"Come on, it's Friday football time. Is Jaden's leg better?"

"Yes, he's fine. He had a good moan about it for a while and limped for a day or two until he forgot to keep pretending it was still hurting. Hang on a minute; I'm just getting my trainers on."

"You'll need them if you want to score another goal," Amber laughed. She had been quite astonished when her friend had kicked that ball so hard a few days ago, but she was also full of admiration for the sheer power of the shot. "I'm sure they'll let you join in today," she joked.

Chaaya had no intention of joining in. She had found out that her ball-kicking *'WHOOSH'* couldn't compete with the golden sound heard in the middle of the night, and it just seemed to be too much hassle to try playing and then be told off by her embarrassed brother again.

On their way to the park Chaaya wondered if she should ask Amber if she had told anyone about the mysterious object but decided it was probably best not to even mention it. However, as they walked along together, Amber brought the subject up herself.

"I see you got rid of the skip."

"What skip?"

"That funny modern skip you had in your back yard. What were you throwing out?"

Chaaya had to think quickly: Amber thought the object had been a kind of waste skip!

"Oh that, yeah, it's gone now. It's not an interesting thing to talk about really, is it?"

But Amber already seemed to have forgotten about it and, always ready for action, she suddenly challenged her friend, "Want to race?"

"Yeah, course I do!"

"First to the swings wins six million pounds. Ready? Go!"

Sally had enjoyed the first part of her mission and had made contact with a few Earth humans. Her plan to act the part of a poor, hungry girl crying for help had given her some insight into Earth human responses to others in need. Three of the four boys who had heard the cry had ignored it, but the fourth had responded with kindness and compassion, and he had unexpectedly been a member of the family that she was concentrating on. The next phase of her mission was about to take place, and Sally wanted to see some of the family members again before the end of the day.

Sitting in her personal caravan, Sally told guinea pig Claude where she was going. "I'm off to see the children at the park again, but remember, you are my best friend and I'll be back soon." Claude was such a good listener and the two of them supported each other in many ways, Sally by providing all he needed and Claude by giving her the kind of love that a small animal can give. The Planet 3 humans were aware that a close relationship with an animal is beneficial to wellbeing, and Professor Xander was glad to encourage his pupils to involve their pets in whatever missions they had chosen; in his own schooldays he had been allowed to take Fiddler, his cat, on his Year 5 summer mission to explore the fungi found in the woodlands of Planet 3's Parkways. (Parkways are the Planet 3 equivalent of National Parks in the UK). On the return to his personal caravan after a long day taking photographs of toadstools, Fiddler would take his mind away from feelings of loneliness and help to keep him happy, simply by being his special cat.

Chaaya and Amber were already at the park when Sally arrived. Chaaya saw her coming through the park entrance and pointed her out to Amber. "Isn't that the girl we saw here last week?"

"I think so. She was sitting on your swing when we got here."

"It's not really my swing."

"When you give me the six million pounds you owe me for winning the race, I'm going to buy both of the swings and the whole park too."

"What did that girl say her name was?"

"She's called Sally, I think, or was it Silly? Oh no, that's your name!"

"Thanks very much, Amber."

"You're welcome."

Sally ran up to them, all smiles. "Hello you two. Do you live right here?"

Chaaya laughed back. "Sometimes it seems like we do." She noticed that, beyond Sally, across the road, Miss Robinson had just come out of her house. Once again, they caught sight of each other, and both waved.

Sally asked, "Is that lady your mum?"

"No, she's my teacher." Chaaya paused.

"I mean she was my teacher, in my last class. She's really special. What's your teacher called?"

"Professor Xander. He's really good."

"He sounds posh to me," said Amber.

Sally didn't really understand what 'posh' meant, but she guessed it might be something good, and replied, "He's the best."

"No," said Chaaya. "He can't be the best because Miss Robinson is."

"I'm sure the professor is the best for me, but Miss Robinson is the best for you." Sally realised she must be careful not to cause an argument, but Chaaya wanted to say just one more thing in Miss Robinson's favour.

"Miss Robinson says she has eyes in the back of her head."

"She can't have!" Chaaya and Amber laughed at their little joke, but Sally didn't join in - in fact Amber noticed that her face seemed to have turned white, like a person who has just seen a ghost.

"I have to go now. Bye," and Sally ran away from them and out of the park as quickly as she could.

"She's a strange person," said Amber, matter-of-factly.

"Oh, she's alright," replied Chaaya. "She just doesn't know us very well, that's all."

Meanwhile, Jaden had noticed Sally coming and going from the park and in a way, he felt relieved that he hadn't spoken to her. He could just imagine

Big Harry asking, "Is that your girlfriend?" and everyone laughing at him. But Jaden also felt pleased: Sally looked well, and she could certainly run, so perhaps she was feeling good again.

The news that Chaaya's teacher had eyes in the back of her head had shocked Sally and she knew she must make a connection with the person known on Earth as Miss Robinson. She wondered if Professor Xander was aware that someone from Planet 3 was living on Earth and acting the part of a teacher. She was also concerned that Miss Robinson might need help in some way. Could she be stranded on Earth, doing her best to survive in the hope that someone from Planet 3 would find her and take her to their personal caravan, eventually getting her back to her true home again?

Back in the safety of her own caravan, Sally told her guinea pig all about it. "I have to go to Miss Robinson's house, Claude. I have to find out the truth." Claude made a deep, relaxed purring sound, meaning, "Please make a fuss of me," and Sally stroked him under his chin. "I'm going to see her tonight in case I have to contact the professor about her." Claude squeaked and lifted his head. He looked directly into Sally's eyes as if trying to say something. "Oh, alright then," she said comfortingly. "We'll have something to eat first!"

8. Who is the Real Miss Robinson?

Sally understood that she would have to be very careful about how she approached Miss Robinson but was excited at the prospect of an unexpected meeting with a fellow Planet 3 human. She was aware that others had visited Earth but had no idea that one could be in such close proximity to her. Similarly, Miss Robinson would have no idea who Sally was, so introductions and revelations would need to be handled with sensitivity. Sally just wanted to give a friendly greeting but wondered if she dare ask Miss Robinson why she had decided to spend such a significant amount of time on Earth. She couldn't be taking part in a teacher exchange because no Earth human had ever discovered the existence of Planet 3, so she must be teaching as part of some kind of grown-up mission. How exciting!

So many thoughts, so many questions and such confident anticipation filled Sally's mind as she approached the house opposite the entrance to the park. It was 6.35 pm, which was a time when many Earth humans seemed to eat a meal, and Sally thought that might be a good time to visit, because few people would be around and there was little chance of anyone overhearing any conversation they might have.

Sally looked all round her. There were just a few older children in the park but no-one else nearby. She approached the front door of Miss Robinson's house and could hear piano music being played inside. Knocking gently didn't have any effect and the piano music continued. But when she knocked a little louder the music stopped and Miss Robinson herself answered the door. She was met by a smiling girl she didn't recognise and asked, "Can I help you?"

"I think so. My name is Sally. I'm very sorry to disturb your lovely playing, Miss Robinson."

There was an awkward moment of silence, until Miss Robinson went on, "Hello, Sally. How do you know my name? I don't think I know you, do I?"

"No, but I'm a friend of Chaaya Williams and she told me that you are her best teacher."

"That was a very nice thing for Chaaya to say." Miss Robinson wondered where this was leading and sensed that Sally needed time to reveal what she had come for.

Sally had planned her next question, which would hopefully lead to further conversation. "I wonder if you have heard of my teacher. His name is Professor Xander. He is very well known where I come from - if you know what I mean."

Miss Robinson scratched her head and thought. "You must be very lucky to be taught by a professor, but I'm sorry to say I don't think I've heard of him."

Sally realised she was going to have to work a little harder. It occurred to her that, if Miss Robinson had come from Planet 3, she had no reason to suspect that Sally was from there too. It was time to begin to slowly reveal her own identity. "Miss Robinson, I have a personal caravan, and I'm staying there with Claude at the moment."

"That's nice, Sally. Is Claude your father?"

Sally laughed. "No, Claude is my guinea pig. My father isn't here, and neither is my mother." Miss Robinson was beginning to wonder if Sally could be in some kind of trouble and decided to listen very carefully to what was being said in case the police or social services would need to be contacted. "Do you see what I'm trying to say, Miss Robinson?"

"I'm listening, Sally. What else do you want to tell me?"

"Miss Robinson, your hair is very similar to mine. I'm wearing a wig. Are you?"

Miss Robinson wondered if Sally had a kind of illness that caused her to lose her hair. A young girl who was ill and living alone in a caravan was going to need a lot of help. Wondering what she might be getting into, she was concerned that something quite serious must have caused the girl to seek help, and that a teacher might be someone who could respond at this difficult moment in her life. "Sally, I'm beginning to understand. Please tell me if I've got this right. You have come to see me because Chaaya told you I am a teacher, and you're trying to tell me that you need help. Is that correct?"

"Sort of. Chaaya told me that you have eyes in the back of your head. That was when I knew I had to see you."

Miss Robinson had often used that phrase but recognised that what Sally was really saying was no laughing matter, so she took care to maintain a serious, concerned tone, and she kindly said, "Having eyes in the back of my head can sometimes help me to help others."

To Sally, that was the proof she needed. Smiling her widest smile, she proudly announced, "I have eyes in the back of my head too." She lifted off her wig and turned round.

At first, Sally couldn't comprehend why Miss Robinson fainted on the spot but then she noticed that, as the teacher toppled over, no wig fell from her head. Gently touching Miss Robinson's hair, Sally realised that she had made a dreadful mistake. Miss Robinson was an Earth human who had been telling a joke!

After feeling greatly relieved that she hadn't caused someone to die of shock, Sally very quickly put her wig back on. Miss Robinson, now sitting up and feeling confused, didn't appear to have suffered any lasting harm.

Sally decided it was time for her to leave and, muttering, "I'm so very, very sorry," she waved, and was pleased to see a puzzled Miss Robinson waving back.

Later that evening, Miss Robinson phoned the police to ask if any suspicious caravans had been seen in the area, but the police said none had been reported. When she then remembered that Sally had said she lived there with a guinea pig she finally convinced herself that the meeting with the girl must not have happened at all and decided that she was simply overtired or possibly remembering a dream. It was time for her to get away for a break, and she booked herself a two-week holiday to Turkey!

9. The Return of the Midnight Grocer

Amber's parents, Laura and Jack, asked Dayana, Jaden and Chaaya to join them for a Friday evening fish and chips supper. It wasn't unusual for the neighbours to eat together, and Friday always seemed like a good time for them to relax and get together for some 'down time' with their friends. Fred's Friendly Fryer, their local chippy, was handily located at the corner of Rankin Street, and Fred had come to expect their usual order of fish and chips six times, two with mushy peas, on Fridays at 6.30 pm.

That evening was a bit of a celebration for Amber's family. Her parents had managed to persuade their manager to let them both have a week off at the same time, and on the Saturday morning they were leaving for a well-deserved holiday at Scarborough on the North Yorkshire coast.

Laura and Jack were acutely aware that Dayana couldn't afford to take time off work for a holiday and so they played down the fun they intended to have at the seaside. As Jack said, "Where we're going the gulls swoop down on the tourists' fish and chips, so think of us fighting them off when you're sitting in the comfort of your own home."

"They're a real menace over there," added Laura. "Some people refuse to eat outside, even in the middle of summer. It's like being attacked by flying vandals when the gulls get going!" Of course, Dayana wished her friends well, saying she hoped they would have a great time and come home without any peck wounds, but secretly she hoped that, just for once, she could find a way to take her children away to the seaside too.

It was almost 11.00 pm when the Williams family got home and fell happily into their beds. Dayana, who would be up early and well on her way to work while the children were still in bed, went straight to sleep, exhausted as usual. Jaden was soon dreaming about scoring the winning goal in the cup final at Wembley Stadium, but Chaaya stayed awake for a while, thinking about spending a week without Amber. It wouldn't be the same to have time away from her, and she wondered if she should look out for Sally, who might want to be friends, even though they had only seen each other very briefly. Chaaya thought Sally could be really nice, but she didn't say much and always seemed to be dashing off. Perhaps she was just shy, Chaaya wondered, and might be keener to spend time with her when Amber was away. Sometimes it's easier to make friends with someone who's on their own rather than with a friend they have known for ages.

Chaaya glanced at the clock. It was just a few minutes to midnight, and she felt herself dozing. She loved that feeling when you know you are going to sleep very soon, and she was about to nod off when, '*WHOOOOOOSH*' - Chaaya suddenly sat up straight. It was that same noise, the sound she thought she had heard at precisely the same time one week ago. This time though, Chaaya knew she hadn't heard it in her sleep, and she also recognised that it wasn't the same sound that the football had made when she kicked it as hard as possible. It was a lovely, incredible sound, like something put together in a professional recording studio for a science fiction film effect. It was also the sound that seemed to be connected in some way to the arrival of the mysterious object last Saturday morning.

Chaaya desperately wanted to see if the 'WHOOOOOOSH' had somehow brought the object back once again, but her bedroom window was at the front of the house. However, her brother's bedroom overlooked the back yard and she wondered if she should sneak in and peep through the curtains while Jaden slept.

Tiptoeing carefully, Chaaya made her way to Jaden's bedroom door. Although it was almost pitch black, she well knew the sign on the door, written in huge letters with a red felt-tip pen that announced, 'JADEN'S ROOM - DANGER - NO ENTRY - RADIOACTIVE WASTE DUMPED HERE - KEEP OUT OR DIE!!!!!!!!' To even touch that door would be far too risky. Jaden deserved his privacy and, if the object really had come back, it would still be there in the morning. Reluctantly, Chaaya returned to her own bed and soon fell into a dream about yellowish-silver aliens who were sitting in the back yard eating packets of crisps.

Chaaya slept until 9.30 am on Saturday, and when she woke, she immediately remembered the '*WHOOOOOOSH*', and her desire to investigate the back yard was still niggling at her. Her mum would have set off for work, and she wondered if Jaden had got up yet. But as soon as she left her room, she could tell that he was still asleep, because she could hear the unmistakable sound of a snoring brother which her mum often referred to as "the hippopotamus in Jaden's room."

Chaaya went downstairs carefully and quietly, taking care not to wake the hippo until she had checked the back yard. She took the back door key from its hook on the kitchen wall and slowly unlocked the door.

There it was!

A shiny yellowish-silver metallic box stood precisely where the shiny yellowish-silver metallic box had been one week ago. Once again, the yard was almost entirely filled by the object. Chaaya couldn't help herself and she let out a cry of excitement and joyful anticipation, then went back into the kitchen and closed the door just so that she could open it and look at what was there once again.

Chaaya wondered if she had woken her brother, and in a way she hoped she had. She wanted to share this moment with someone, and the fact that Jaden hadn't believed her when she told him what happened last week made her feel excited that he would soon find out the truth for himself. She went to the bottom of the stairs and listened. Was Jaden awake? She thought he could be because the hippopotamus couldn't be heard. Just as she was about to call Jaden's name she saw, out of the corner of her eye, that a small thin packet, no more than ten centimetres long and wrapped in a yellowish-silver material, had been pushed through the letter box in the front door. Knowing precisely what that meant, Chaaya picked up the packet. As before, it felt quite metallic, but it was simple to tear it open. A short, thin yellowish-silver object fell onto the floor. When she picked it up Chaaya felt its familiar smoothness and warmth, which was quite comforting in a strange way. She knew what it was of course, it was a warm, magical pencil wand, which was some form of key that opened the object containing their weekly shopping.

"What's all that noise?" Jaden appeared at the top of the stairs.

"What do you mean?"

"You made a noise like a cat fight outside my window."

"Come down here, I want to show you something."

"Will it take long? I need to get ready for football and I haven't eaten anything yet."

Chaaya laughed. "What I'm going to show you will make you forget about football!"

"Impossible." But Jaden knew his sister well, and something in her tone of voice caused him to go downstairs to see what the fuss was about. "Right, I'm here. Let's get on with it."

"Follow me." Chaaya could have simply asked Jaden to open the back door, but she wanted to lead him there as if she owned a secret that she was going to reveal, which in a way she was.

She paused by the back door, holding the handle. Then, with a flourish and a grin, she opened the door. Jaden looked, silently at first. Then his mouth slowly opened wide, the bottom jaw dropping as he let out a yelping sound, "Fffooaaarrrr! What is it?"

"It's what Mum and I both told you about last week."

"It's real!"

"It's real alright, and I know what's in it."

"No, you don't because you can't get in it, there's no door. It's just a big lump of metal, like a.... like a.... big lump of metal."

It was time for the magic show. Chaaya held up the pencil-like object. "And now, the magic word," she announced and, waving the wand, she mysteriously said the first thing that came into her mouth, "Hello, midnight grocer." The huge object and the small pencil wand both instantly vanished as the back yard revealed the treasure that took their place.

The siblings reacted with utter astonishment, and they both exclaimed, "I don't believe it!" at precisely the same moment. Chaaya had expected to see a repeat of the previous week's surprise, that being the weekly shopping. It was indeed there as before, but so were lots of other piles of weekly shopping and two additional baskets of fruit and vegetables.

Chaaya was lost for words, but Jaden gasped, "Is this all for us?"

"I guess so."

"Where are we going to put it all?"

"I don't know. Let's wait until Mum gets home."

During the next few minutes Chaaya counted the number of sets of weekly shopping that the two of them arranged in neat, tidy, identical piles in the back yard. There were thirty sets, enough for the family to use and enjoy for thirty weeks. Jaden took one complete set into the kitchen and arranged the food on one of the surfaces. As before, among all the usual items their mum would normally have bought from the supermarket, there were two chocolate oranges.

Jaden was absolutely astonished. His sister and mother hadn't made up an incredibly unbelievable story last week - it was all true. And Chaaya was right about something else; Jaden had forgotten all about playing football, but there was something else on his mind. Picking up his chocolate orange he headed to the front door. "I'll be back soon," he called and, before Chaaya had time to ask where he was going, he ran off in the direction of the alleyway to Paradise Street.

10. Cardboard Nest

As soon as Jaden caught sight of that chocolate orange he thought of Sally, the girl he had found in the back yard of number 2 Paradise Street. He had also seen her at the park but had no idea where she might be living and didn't want to ask Chaaya if she knew anything about her. He wanted his act of kindness towards the girl to be his secret. Now that he had possession of another chocolate orange, he felt strongly that he should give it to Sally. The last time he saw her in the park she looked well enough, but what if she now felt the same unhappiness that he had seen the previous weekend?

As usual, Jaden ran quickly down Rankin Street and around the corner to the alleyway leading to the back of Paradise Street. He stopped in his tracks when he got there and listened carefully for about a minute. He could hear no crying, which he thought must be a good thing. Should he choose to go home now, remembering that he and many other young people had been warned not to go into that alleyway? If he chose to go straight back home, he could eat the chocolate orange himself, which is what he would love to do. Or should he peep into the back yard of number 2 just in case Sally was there, in need of more food or support?

Jaden found himself doing what he always knew he was going to do. He crept very slowly into the alleyway. After listening for a few more seconds and hearing nothing, he peeped into the back yard of number 2. There didn't appear to be any sign that Sally had been there recently, but he did hear something. A low groaning sound reminded him of a polar bear he had seen on television. It was coming from a large heap of flattened cardboard boxes in the corner behind him. Jaden had noticed the cardboard pile on his last visit and didn't think it meant anything important, but this time he looked at it more closely. He guessed that a dog must have somehow got underneath the boxes, so he gently said, "Hello, come here, come on."

To his great surprise, a man's voice replied. "Who are you?" and the boxes moved one way and then the other as first two hands, then two arms and finally a hairy head appeared. Jaden, rooted to the spot with fear, said nothing.

Realising that he must look terrifying to any child, the man spoke again. "Did you think I was a dog?"

"Yeah. Sorry, really sorry."

"No need to be sorry, kiddo. Hey, I won't hurt you, wouldn't hurt a fly." Jaden realised that the man spoke with a different accent than his own and wondered if he was from Jamaica because it reminded him of one of his heroes, Usain Bolt. "Thank you for coming again."

"Again?" Jaden was confused.

"You came last week and saw the girl, but you didn't see me. I kept still and quiet, but I could tell you were a good lad, helping her like that." There was a pause and the man continued. "By the way, I'm Carl. This is my home," and he waved an arm to indicate the heap of cardboard. "They say people like me are sleeping rough, but I say I'm in my cardboard nest."

Although Jaden remembered that he had been told to be careful when approached by strangers, he realised that it was he who was doing the approaching, wandering into Carl's territory and he asked, "Has the girl been here since last week?"

"Not as far as I know."

Jaden realised he was still holding the chocolate orange. Feeling awkward, but also guessing that Carl was probably just as much in need of support as Sally, he heard himself asking, "Would you like some chocolate?"

Carl scratched his head, pretending to be deep in thought but grinning too. "Well go on then', he said. "I'll share it with you, kiddo."

Jaden opened the wrapper and stretched out his hand. The man reached towards it and took half of the chocolate segments. "Thank you, kiddo. Hey, I can't keep calling you that. What's your name?"

Jaden hesitated. He liked the man and was sure he wasn't going to do him any harm, but he didn't think it was wise or clever to give his real name, so he said the first one that came into his head, "I'm Usain."

"A fine and famous name, a name to be proud of." Carl finished the chocolate and said, "Eat up, Usain, my boy."

Without further thought, Jaden put the rest of the chocolate orange, still in its wrapper, on a flat bit of cardboard near the man's hand. "It's for you." He moved slowly away from the man, and saying no more, waved and turned to leave.

"You're a good person, Usain. Thank you for coming to see me."

Jaden could feel his heart beating quickly, but he also felt a surge of happiness, similar to when he had helped Sally. With a spring in his step and a big smile on his face he headed back home to Chaaya.

11. So Much Food!

Chaaya couldn't begin to imagine what they were going to do with all the groceries, and she was so relieved when Jaden came back. She was worried that the scary gulls Amber and her dad had spoken about might swoop over the back yard, grab all the food into their beaks and fly off with it.

Together, the Williams children carried all the food into the house. Thirty sets of weekly shopping must be put somewhere, and after another hour they had been placed carefully into every room in the house. "I don't know whether to laugh or to cry," said Chaaya, despairingly. "What are we going to do with all this food?"

Jaden didn't have an answer. They looked at each other and both said at exactly the same time, "Wait till Mum gets home!"

By mid-morning, Sally was wondering whether the Williams family had found their thirty sets of weekly shopping and, if so, how they had reacted. This was an interesting moment in her mission, and she was intrigued to know what would happen. Frustratingly, she had been told many times that she must not interfere with whatever choices the family might make. To interact with the Earth humans was fine - in fact it was positively encouraged, but if she were to go to their home immediately after the arrival of one of the silvercrates, her entire mission would be deemed invalid because she could have influenced the family's decisions. However, Sally wasn't worried that Jaden's response to her well-acted tears would be frowned upon by the professor, because there was no way of knowing who, if anyone, would go to her aid; the fact that a member of the family she was studying was the only one to respond had come as a surprise to her, and she had given no reason for Jaden to link her to the silvercrates or the weekly shopping.

Sally spent much of the day in her personal caravan, playing computer games and enjoying spending time with her special friend Claude.

Dayana had been concerned that, because she had to go to work and the Hodgson family were away on holiday, her children would need alternative childcare of some sort. She told them to phone her every hour, on the hour, to let her know they were all right. However, that wasn't enough to guarantee their safety, so she asked Shahid Nanda, another neighbour, if he would mind calling to see them briefly but regularly every day.

Living at number 28, Shahid was a sensible young man who was currently out of work. He had left school after doing well in his A-levels but didn't feel that university life would suit him. After a year of travelling across many Asian countries with a bag on his back and a willingness to work whenever and wherever he could find it, he moved in with a friend, sharing the rent for the house in Rankin Street while studying for an Open University degree. Dayana considered Shahid to be totally reliable, and he was happy to help look after the children. The arrangement made with Dayana was that he would knock on the Williams' door at half past every hour and see if the children needed anything. Shahid was happy to go outside with the two youngsters if he had the time and hoped they would like to do that.

Shahid called, as promised, on the Saturday morning. He was surprised that the children didn't seem to want to go outside at all, but they had come to the window and despite not opening the curtains they let him know they were busy. Of course, the curtains were drawn because they didn't want Shahid or anyone else to see the vast quantity of food that filled every room.

After Chaaya and Jaden had finished moving all the food, all still in its original sets of weekly shopping, they showered, dressed and eventually had a very late breakfast before talking about what could be happening to them. They were left with a situation that was lovely in some ways but problematic in others. There were so many unanswered questions, and the thing that puzzled them most was who could be leaving all this food in their back yard and why. They considered all the possibilities: perhaps a kind friend would turn up later and explain everything –

or could it be a brilliant magician practising for the greatest trick of all time? Chaaya continued to insist that a mysterious figure she liked to refer to as "the midnight grocer" was behind it all.

When Shahid knocked at 1.30 pm he was pleased that both Jaden and Chaaya came out to see him. They already had their outdoor clothes on, so Shahid asked, "Where shall we go?"

Jaden was aware that by now his friends would have already been playing football and hanging out together for hours and he would feel a bit silly if he turned up late, but he really wanted to play football for a while, so he asked Shahid, "Do you fancy a kickabout?"

"Hang on a minute," said Chaaya. "What about me?"

"No problem," said Shahid. "We can all play together." Jaden grimaced in Chaaya's direction, and she playfully stuck her tongue out at him. Jaden went back into the house and came out with the football that he had left inside the front door 'just in case', and Shahid texted Dayana to let her know they would call her when they got home rather than while they were playing.

The three of them walked about a mile to a grassy area in front of the local swimming baths. The space wasn't big enough for an organised match, but was just right for a kickabout for three friends. Shahid put down his coat to represent one goalpost and, about four metres away, his hat to be the other and said, "I'll go in goal for ten minutes, you two pass the ball around and take shots at me, then it's someone else's turn to go in goal."

As he kicked the ball in her direction Chaaya realised that this was the first time she had actually played football with Jaden, and she loved everything about it. She really enjoyed passing to her brother and watching him shoot, and felt so special when he passed to her, but most of all she loved it when she could hit a powerful shot at goal, enjoy the '*WHOOSH*' and celebrate a goal.

Ten minutes later it was Jaden's turn to be in goal, and Chaaya had more shots than ever because Shahid was happy to set her up most of the time.

Jaden saved many of her attempts but when she did score, she felt a thrill to see the ball go past such a good goalkeeper. She didn't enjoy her ten-minute spell in goal, but knew it was important to take turns and it was soon time for Shahid to replace her anyway.

A couple of hours in the warm summer afternoon sun seemed to fly by, and they set off home tired but very happy, all three of them having had a good time. At 4.00 pm, just before they got home, Jaden phoned their mum and Chaaya heard him say something surprising that meant such a lot to her, "Yeah, we had a great afternoon. We played football with Shahid, and Chaaya was brilliant!" Hearing her own brother, the goalscorer-supreme, say those words, Chaaya felt her heart leap with joy. She was so overcome that she hardly heard Jaden add, "Yeah, it's good that you're able to get home early, Mum. See you in twenty minutes."

"Why are you crying, Mum?" Chaaya knew her mother would be overwhelmed by many mixed emotions when she saw such an abundance of riches in her own home, but she hated to see her cry. Dayana had been so happy to go home early for once, but her astonishment at finding the house looking like a supermarket storage unit, combined with the worry that she was going to have to think of somewhere to put everything, had left her feeling completely exhausted.

Chaaya took control of the situation. "I'll put the kettle on, Mum."

"Who is doing this to us?" It was Dayana's turn to ask that obvious question.

Jaden tried to lighten the situation. "Look Mum, we don't understand why somebody has left all this stuff for us, but we won't need to buy any food for thirty weeks!"

The initial shock that had caused Dayana's tears was subsiding. She understood Jaden's sentiments but dismissed them. "Listen to me, both of you." Chaaya came back from starting to make the tea and sat alongside her mother and Jaden. "Most of this food is not ours. Maybe one lot of weekly shopping is for us, but not all of it. We must share it with other people. We don't have much money and I have to spend just about everything I earn to get us what we need, so we should be grateful that somebody wants to look after us, but the rest of it…" Dayana stopped talking and gave a big sigh.

A sudden realisation came to Chaaya. "I've got it!" she cried, jumping up. There are thirty sets of shopping - how many houses are there in Rankin Street?"

Jaden also leapt up. "Thirty!"

"That's it then," exclaimed Dayana. "There's one weekly shop for every house."

The two hours that followed were incredible. Working together, the three members of the Williams family carefully put one set of weekly shopping into each of many bags, boxes and wrapped up newspapers they could find. They then set off out together, taking one lot of weekly shopping to each of the houses in Rankin Street except the Hodgson's home. "We can save theirs for when they get back from Scarborough," explained Dayana. They knocked on each door in turn, if someone answered, one of them would simply say, "This is for you." If asked why they were giving such a gift they would answer, "Because you deserve it," and quickly leave. If no-one answered their knock, they would leave the food in the back yard "Just like it happened to us," said Chaaya.

When the sets of weekly shopping had been delivered as planned, three tired but very happy people came home and just flopped into their seats.

"That was fantastic!" exclaimed Chaaya, and they all cheered spontaneously.

"Hang on a minute," joked Dayana. "Hasn't that kettle boiled yet?"

12. Concern for Claude

Two days had passed since the family distributed the weekly shopping packs. A lot of people in the street were talking about their gratitude to Dayana and the children for sharing such a lot. None of them really believed that Dayana could have paid for all of it herself, but they didn't think it was polite to ask her who was behind it all. They assumed that the gift was a 'one-off', and for that they were all grateful.

Chaaya was enjoying her school holiday. The summer weather was great, and she was having fun with Jaden; the kickabout with Shahid seemed to have brought the siblings closer together and they were having a lot of laughs. Shahid himself was great company. He remembered what it was like to be their age and seemed to enjoy a chance to join in with them as a break from his studies.

But Chaaya felt that something that wasn't quite right. Since Amber had gone away, she hadn't contacted any of the other girls from school, and she wondered if there could be a chance that Sally might like to spend a bit of time with her. Sally seemed to be a pleasant girl, but there was something about her that made her seem different. Chaaya suspected that Sally could be a shy person, but perhaps she was looking for a friend too…

Sally was actually quite worried. That morning she noticed that Claude hadn't eaten his pellets and had drunk hardly any water. She offered him a piece of cucumber from the Eco-tech fresh vegetable system, but he refused it. When Sally picked him up, he didn't make his usual happy sounds and she thought his tummy felt a bit tubbier than usual. Putting Claude into his special adventure playground didn't help either; he usually loved running round the circuit but today he just didn't move. Sally's priority was to look after Claude. But how could she help him to get better? Only one option was available to her, and that would mean involving the family she had come to study.

Sally was delighted to find a little cardboard pet-carrying box in the personal caravan's main cupboard. Professor Xander had thought of everything! She put some hay in the box along with the cucumber and told Claude what was about to happen. "Now, my little friend, you and I are going to have a walk together." Claude still made no sound, which wasn't like him at all, and Sally knew she would have to take action without further delay. "Let's go and find someone to help you get well again." And, holding the pet-carrying box and its precious load, she headed toward Rankin Street.

It suddenly occurred to Sally that she wasn't supposed to tell the Williams family that she knew their address. She was about to return to her personal caravan for a re-think when she saw two boys crossing the road towards her. She had seen them playing football with Jaden and decided to approach them. "Excuse me," she said, looking in their direction.

Baz and Big Harry stopped. "Excuse me too," said Baz. "I can be as posh as you."

Not understanding Baz's attempt at a joke, Sally continued. "Please can you tell me where Chaaya Williams lives?"

"What's it worth?"

"What do you mean?"

"I mean what will you give me if I tell you? Can I have what's in that box?"

Big Harry realised that Sally was confused by Baz's silly question, and he intervened, saying, "Leave it, Baz." He turned to Sally and said, "She lives just up that street, number 28."

At last, thought Sally, someone who doesn't speak in riddles. "Thank you," she said as she turned to head towards Chaaya's house.

"Sometimes, Baz," said Big Harry, "the things you say to others are just plain nasty."

"Sometimes," replied Baz, "you irritate me. I was only having a laugh with her. No harm in that, is there?"

In a few moments Sally was knocking on the door of 24 Rankin Street, hoping Chaaya would be at home, but it was Jaden who answered the door. Seeing Sally standing there, he went straight outside to talk to her, closing the door behind him. He quickly asked, "Are you alright?" He was baffled to see the girl he had helped in Paradise Street standing there and wondered how he was going to explain himself to Chaaya.

"Yes," said Sally, "I'm fine, but my guinea pig is ill, and I hope you or Chaaya can help me decide if I need to take him home or not."

Jaden felt relieved, not because Sally's guinea pig was ill but because there was a way he could be seen with Sally without explaining himself to his sister. "Chaaya's up in her room," he explained. "I'll tell her you're here, but can you do something for me?" Before Sally could answer, he continued, "Please can we both pretend that this is the first time we have met?" Sally nodded, and Jaden opened the door, beckoning her to come into the front room.

Jaden called up from the bottom of the stairs, "Chaaya, someone called Sally is here to see you."

Chaaya almost jumped for joy, and bounded downstairs. "How did you find me?" she asked.

"Two of your brother's friends told me where you lived," replied Sally.

"Which friends?" asked Jaden.

"One was tall with wide shoulders and the other was a bit sarcastic." Jaden laughed and nodded, instantly knowing who Sally was talking about.

"I'm glad they did," said Chaaya. Then, noticing the pet-carrying box, she added, "What's in the box?"

Sally opened the box and gently held her precious friend. "This is Claude," she said quietly, "and I'm afraid he's not very well."

Chaaya and Jaden were so pleased to see a guinea pig in their own home. They had both always hoped that one day they might have a pet to care for themselves. After a stroke from each of them, to which Claude didn't really respond much at all, Sally talked about her difficulty. She explained that her parents were a long way away but that they would want her to take Claude to see a vet. Chaaya didn't know where the vet's surgery might be, but Jaden felt sure that Shahid, being older and with more knowledge of such things, would know. Before any more precious time could be wasted, Jaden ran to number 28 and Shahid hurried to join them. He took one look at Claude and agreed that expert help was needed.

The vet's surgery was almost two miles away on the other side of town, and all four of them were quite tired by the time they got there. They hadn't exactly been running, because Claude's box had to be held as still as possible, but they felt as if they had at least been in a walking race when finally arriving at the reception desk. Shahid, being the adult of the party, did most of the talking. The receptionist asked him to fill in a form, and he did so without speaking to Sally as he didn't want her to be too worried when he described Claude's symptoms. When he got to the section that asked for name, address, and signature he filled it in with his own details. The receptionist asked them all to sit in the waiting room and, within ten minutes, she took them through to the treatment room where small animal vet, Jan Norman, met them with a smile. Sally liked her straight away and loved the way she spoke to Claude.

"Let's have a good look at you, sir. You are a fine looking gentlepig, aren't you?" Her voice was soothing and full of care. Sally told her all about Claude, explaining that he was about one year old, was a great friend, always loved to play and normally ate well. Jan asked her how long it had been since she first noticed that Claude was not eating and was pleased to hear that Sally said it was only since that morning. "You have brought him here in good time so well done," said Jan. "I think I know what we need to do to make him better, so there's no need to worry."

Sally was very relieved. She trusted Jan to tell her the truth and listened carefully to what she was explaining. "Guinea pigs are herbivores, so their diet should be one based on high-quality guinea pig hay, pelleted guinea pig food and limited amounts of fresh vegetables and fresh fruit."

"Those are the things he always eats," said Sally.

"I'm sure you look after him well," continued Jan. "He's very lucky to have you. At the moment he is a little bloated. He needs to carry on eating the good high fibre foods you give him, but he's feeling off his food. I'm going to give him some medicine that will help him now, and I'd like you to give him some more of it twice a day using a little dropper. Please also make sure he has plenty of fresh, clean water because that will help to flush his system and reduce the gas in his tummy."

Sally had a sudden thought. Perhaps the Eco-tech fresh vegetable system in her personal caravan wasn't working properly, or perhaps Claude needed better quality water, could it be that the technology providing air, water and food for humans in her personal caravan wasn't quite right for guinea pigs?

Jan Norman showed Sally how to give Claude his medicine and explained that she was confident he would get better in a few days if he got plenty of fresh water, clean air and good food. Sally was concerned that she might not be able to provide exactly what he was going to need.

After lots of reassurance from Jan and many thanks to her in return, the four friends went back into the waiting room. They were about to start the two mile walk home when the receptionist beckoned Shahid over to her. Although they were a few metres away from the reception desk, the children could hear that Shahid was being asked to pay £32 for the consultation and treatment. Sally was horrified; £32 was approximately 8 sperglons, and she couldn't pay! Not only that but, if Professor Xander were to ask her parents for the money, they would struggle to afford it. Shahid took out his wallet and was about to remove the money when Jan Norman suddenly came to the desk. She could see what Shahid was doing and looked angrily at the receptionist. "I'm sorry, Mr Nanda - you shouldn't have been asked to pay."

"It's not a problem," replied Shahid.

But Jan was insistent. "I realise that Sally isn't your daughter and that Claude belongs to her. You have been kind enough to bring Claude and the children to me, and there will be no charge for Sally. She has done the right thing by going to you, Mr Nanda, and I'm just happy to be able to help too."

Sally ran to the desk. "Thank you, thank you," she said to Jan, "from me and from Claude!"

13. The Palace

Shahid led the group home, keeping everyone's spirits up by telling them about his own pets and their adventures. He, his three sisters and a brother had had a total of eight guinea pigs, six cats and two dogs between them, and he suggested that the occasional spider that appeared in their bath might also count as a pet. After all, he told them, the spiders that came to live in the house always seemed to be happy - he had never heard one complain. Shahid could tell that Sally was worried about Claude and he tried to reassure her by letting her know that lots of pets have times when they don't feel well, just like humans, but that vets are brilliant people who know exactly what to do to make them better. But something else was also on Sally's mind…

Shahid had phoned Dayana before leaving the vet's surgery, letting her know where they had all gone that afternoon, because he knew she would get back home before them.

Chaaya loved being able to introduce Sally to their mum and Dayana was pleased to know that her children had helped Sally to take Claude to the vet. "My word, he's a fine fellow," Dayana said, peeping through the gaps in the top of the pet carrying box. "I'm sure he'll soon be back to full health with someone as caring as you taking care of him, Sally."

"I'll do my best, Mrs Williams."

Dayana looked all round, as if trying to see who Sally was talking to. "Who's this Mrs Williams? Please call me Dayana."

"Oh, that's lovely, thank you, Dayana," replied Sally. "As I said, I'll do my best but I'm not sure my best will be good enough."

"Why ever not, dear?"

"I'm away from home at the moment and where I'm staying, I can't give Claude fresh air or the best water."

Dayana thought for a moment, then beckoned to Shahid. "Please could you give me a hand? There's something up in the loft that might be useful." At the top of the stairs was a door in the ceiling, leading up to a small loft. Dayana hadn't been up there for years but still remembered how to open it with a special stick. As the door opened a ladder extended down to the floor. "Do you think you could pop up there for me, Shahid? It's quite dark, but if you reach round to the right, you might find what Sally needs for Claude."

A few moments later Shahid and Dayana reappeared downstairs. Shahid was carrying a kind of large wooden box with a door covered in wire mesh at the front.

"It's a rabbit hutch!" declared Chaaya.

"And a rabbit hutch will be like a palace for a guinea pig. Sally, would you like Claude to stay here for a while, until he gets better?" Dayana's question filled Sally with happiness.

She had been very worried that there might not be the best fresh air or good quality water in the personal caravan, and Dayana was now offering the best solution in order to provide Claude with just what he needed. Dayana continued, "We would love to have a guest living with us for a while, wouldn't we, children?" Chaaya and Jaden were clearly in agreement, they could hardly believe that they would have the chance to help look after a real pet at last and they gave their mum big smiles. "It's lovely weather, so Claude can live in his palace in the back yard. Sally, it would be lovely if you could stay here too, but we don't have any spare rooms in our little house. You can come here as often as you like, though!"

"Please can I come to give him his medicine?" asked Sally.

"You're the expert, dear. Of course, you can."

Needless to say, everyone was happy with the arrangement. Sally set off to the personal caravan to bring Claude's pellets, hay, and fresh vegetables, and Shahid, after being thanked by everyone again, went back to his own home.

Chaaya was puzzled and, now that just the three of them were in the house, she wanted to ask Dayana something. "Mum, we didn't know there was a hutch in the loft. Why was it there?"

There was a long pause before Dayana replied, and what she said came as a complete surprise to both the children. "Your dad made it." She stopped talking and sat down.

Jaden was the next to speak. "What dad? We don't have a dad, do we?"

"Everyone has a father or had a father at some point."

"Yeah, but,"

Chaaya interrupted. "Will you tell us about him, Mum?"

Once again there was a moment of silence. After what seemed like many minutes but was in reality only twenty seconds or so, Dayana quietly agreed. "Alright, I will, but after we have eaten some more of our lovely weekly shop."

Sally returned with everything Claude would need during his stay with the Williams family. Jaden helped her to carry the hutch outside, and Claude was soon slowly exploring his luxury palace. After giving him his medicine, Sally gave each of her new friends a hug and returned to her personal caravan. She felt much better about Claude now, knowing that with a lot of kindness and the best treatment, he should soon be back to being his familiar happy self once again.

The mealtime was quieter than usual. Dayana was pensive, lost in thought, as she put together in her head what she could say in answer to Chaaya's question. She knew that the time had come to tell the truth about her husband, and suddenly wondered why she had been putting it off for so long. Jaden and Chaaya were also both deep in thought - the revelation that they had actually had a dad, a real person who once made a rabbit hutch, made them excited but also a bit scared of what their mum was going to tell them. Of course, everyone has to have had a father, but they had become sort of comfortable with the old truth.

"Let's all sit down together," began Dayana gently, and she sat in the middle of the two-seater settee so that Jaden and Chaaya could sit either side of her. She put her arms around them both. "Your dad was a good man. He lived here with me when Jaden was born. He was so excited to be a father and built the rabbit hutch before Jaden was six months old. He always wanted to surprise you with a rabbit for your first Christmas, Jaden. We had some smashing times here, walking out with the pushchair, showing you off to the rest of the street and being together as a family."

"What about me?" asked Chaaya.

Dayana laughed and gently explained, "You hadn't been born."

"Oh, I wish I'd been here then."

"You don't get to have a say in when you are going to be born! Anyway, your dad wasn't feeling well. I didn't realise he was doing things that were making him ill, but he became really quiet and sort of sad."

Jaden thought he knew what his mum meant. "Was he taking drugs?"

"Something like that. The doctor didn't seem able to help him, and his mental health was really bad. He told me he was going away to get help. I asked him to stay over and over again, but he said he was bad for me and for you too, Jaden. He left one day when we were both out. I don't know where he went. I phoned the police and they tried to find him but eventually I realised it was like looking for a needle in a haystack. I still don't know where he is. The truth is I don't even know if he's alive. I'm convinced that by leaving he thought he was actually showing us that he loved us, and he somehow believed that we would be better off without him around."

Confused, Chaaya couldn't understand how she fitted into the story, but her mum continued, "He's your dad too, but you were born about seven months after he left. He didn't know about you." Chaaya started to sob, partly for herself but mainly for the other two and for the father she never knew. Needless to say, the three of them had 'a good cry' together.

Dayana was the next to speak. "Can you see now why it's easier to say you don't have a dad?" They both nodded.

"But you know what?" Chaaya pointed out. "Nothing has changed, has it? We have… us!"

Jaden leapt to his feet. "Yes, and tonight we have a guest guinea pig in our dad's palace. Let's all go and see him before we go to bed."

14. Cucumber, Banana and Crisps

The friendship between Chaaya, Jaden and Sally grew stronger every day. Looking after Claude became a three-person job, and they all took turns in giving him his medicine, changing his water, and trying to help him show an interest in food. Progress was slow for the first two days, but by Thursday it was obvious that he was gradually feeling better because he started making some happy noises and even bit into a piece of cucumber. On the Friday he moved around the hutch more quickly and everyone could see that the bloating was improving.

Sally carefully managed to avoid going into detail about where she lived. She didn't want to tell lies, but it was important to say as little as possible about her home life. If she were to even hint that she had come from Planet 3 she would be laughed at, so it was better to say nothing at all about it. The Williams family understood that Sally was staying away from home for a while but that she was well looked after, so assumed she was staying with friends or relatives in the area and that they didn't really need to know any more than that.

Shahid was a great friend of the family. It was so good to get to know him even better, both as a kind of part-time carer for Chaaya and Jaden and as a person who loved to join in the fun of the school holiday. The first time Sally was asked if she would like to go for a kickabout with the three of them she worried that her wig might come off during the physical activity but decided to tell Chaaya that she wore one because she had no hair (which was true), and Chaaya lent her a headband. Chaaya quietly confided in the others about Sally's lack of hair, and they accepted it as a fact with no need to pry any further into their friend's privacy.

Other than looking after Claude and playing kickabout football, the days were spent going to the park, watching TV, playing indoor games including some on Shahid's laptop that he allowed them to borrow when he wasn't using it and generally just being together. On the Thursday afternoon, when the temperature reached over thirty degrees Celsius, they had a long and hilarious water fight, using such weapons as water pistols, a hosepipe and balloons. All of them, including Shahid, were soaked to the skin but soon dried out afterwards in the intense heat, sitting on the low wall in front of Shahid's house and eating ice creams that he bought for everyone.

Jaden was having such a great time playing with the others and looking after Claude that he didn't see his football friends for a few days. Of course, he still loved playing with them and knew he would be doing that again before long, but the time spent at home was suddenly more special than usual. He didn't forget though, that Carl was living in a pile of cardboard boxes not far away. He wouldn't be having fun playing water squirting games and football or guinea pig minding, and Jaden wanted to go to see him again.

On the Friday afternoon, with Claude recovering so well, the girls playing a card game and Shahid reading a psychology book in their front room, Jaden decided to go back to number 2 Paradise

Street. He told the others he was just popping out for half an hour, picked up a packet of crisps and a banana from the kitchen and set off to see if Carl was there.

Again, Jaden ran to the alleyway leading to Paradise Street before stopping and listening. All was quiet so he slowly tiptoed to the back of number 2. He was surprised to see Carl sitting on the ground next to his cardboard nest. "Hey Usain, how's yourself?"

"Hello, Carl. I brought you something." Jaden handed over the banana and the packet of crisps. Carl put them down beside him and Jaden, suddenly unsure what else to say, added, "I hope you like them."

"I do like them, yeah. But Usain, why are you so kind to me?"

Jaden hadn't expected to be asked that question. He didn't know how to reply and mumbled, "I guess I just wanted to be helpful."

Peeling the banana, Carl said, "Helpful must be your middle name." They both laughed. Carl finished the banana in a few seconds and opened the crisp packet. "Hey, Usain, have some crisps with me."

"No, they're for you."

Carl hesitated, then ate the whole packet. "You're a good fella, Usain. Your parents must be very proud of you."

Embarrassed, Jaden muttered, "Thank you."

"And thank you too, thank you very much, but," Carl paused and suddenly looked very serious. "Usain, I'm not the worst off, you know. From here to the far end of this street there are at least fifteen others."

"Others?" Jaden's eyes suddenly flickered in all directions. "Where are they all?"

"In different places, mainly back yards like me. Some come and go, but some of them stay around. And Usain, I have to tell you that I'm better off than all the others."

"I had no idea…" Jaden was shocked to hear what Carl was saying and he wasn't sure how to react to it.

"Do you want me to take you to meet them?"

Jaden suddenly felt very scared. Going into Paradise Street without his mum's permission was a calculated risk, but the prospect of being taken to meet others who were worse off than Carl sounded like a step too far. However, Jaden really wanted to prove himself as a deeply caring person, not only to Carl but to himself and he had an idea. "Can I bring someone with me?"

Carl looked concerned at the prospect of letting others know about the rough sleepers, and he quickly asked, "Who would the other person be?"

"I have an older friend, a man called Shahid. He's a great guy. Can I ask him to come?"

Carl suddenly looked quite alarmed. "Is he a policeman?"

"No, he's a kind of older student who looks after me sometimes."

"I don't know, Usain. I'll have to think about it. You can go home now." Jaden felt that he had upset Carl in some way. Of course, he hadn't meant to, and he realised that Carl meant him no harm, but he had to be responsible for his own safety. Nevertheless, being told to go came as a shock and he suddenly felt that Carl might not want any further contact with him.

Left alone again, Carl thought that he might have been wrong to invite Usain to meet the other rough sleepers. He had tried to make it clear that the others were worse off than him, but what he had also wanted to say was that maybe someone could help him to find a way of making things better for the Paradise Street community. He really needed experienced adult support if any progress could be made, and Usain was probably the wrong person to have told, but he had no other contacts. After much thought, Carl hoped that the boy would return, with or without the older friend.

That evening, Dayana noticed that Jaden was strangely quiet. When Chaaya and Sally were busy playing with Claude, she beckoned him into the kitchen and quietly asked, "Are you okay?"

Jaden seemed quite defensive, replying, "Why are you asking me that?" in a moody tone.

"You just seem to be a bit quiet, so I thought I'd ask. Is something upsetting you?"

"No. I'm just thinking."

"I suppose there's a first time for everything!" Dayana made him laugh, and he was secretly pleased that she had helped him to stop thinking about what Carl had said. He bounced back to the front room to see what the girls were getting up to. Sally was putting her shoes on, and when she saw that everyone was there, she said, "Thank you for a great time and for looking after Claude. I won't be able to see you for a couple of days, but I'll be back soon."

The disappointed faces in the room told her how much they all enjoyed her friendship, and she had a lovely warm feeling inside. "Should I take Claude with me until I get back or would you like him to stay here?"

Chaaya answered immediately, "Oh, could he stay here please? We'll look after him well and when you get back you'll see a much healthier guinea pig!"

Sally skipped off happily down the street. She loved being a temporary part of the Williams family and wished she could be with them for the whole of her last week on Earth. But she knew that she wouldn't be able to be there during the coming hours, when the third silvercrate, leading to the final part of her mission, would arrive in their back yard.

15. Squeaks and Whooshes

Dayana decided to ask the children to help her carry the hutch containing Claude into the kitchen before they went to bed. She hated to think what could happen to the palace and its precious resident if delivery of another huge object were to take place for a third consecutive Friday at midnight. As they carried the hutch inside, they all heard excited guinea pig squeaks. "He's thrilled about spending the night in the house," Chaaya chortled.

"I think it means he's feeling a lot better too," added Jaden.

Now that Dayana had raised the subject of who or what Chaaya referred to as the "midnight grocer", they decided that they would all get up at 7.30 am, giving Dayana time to see if anything had arrived and, if so, what was inside the object. All three fell asleep early that night, but they were all awakened at midnight by what Chaaya later described as, "The loudest '*WHOOOOOOSH*' of all!" Such was the excitement and anticipation of what they might find in the morning that they didn't get back to sleep for a while. Jaden now understood why Chaaya thought the sound reminded her of football, and he wondered how loud the '*WHOOOSH*' would be if he could actually kick a ball all the way up into the clouds.

All three members of the family were standing in the kitchen, tired but excited, at 7.32 am. Chaaya was holding the third warm pencil wand from within the small packet she had again found just inside the front door. Dayana turned the key in the lock, opened the back door and, oh yes, there it was – the now familiar shiny yellowish-silver metallic box, but this one appeared to have something written on it in huge blue letters. Jaden quickly leapt on top of it to see what the writing said. Each letter was at least thirty centimetres high. Jaden read the words out loud, "It says, 'THIS IS YOUR FINAL DELIVERY. THANK YOU.'"

"Hasn't anyone signed that message?" Dayana asked.

"No, that's all it says."

"So, we might never know where they have been coming from."

Chaaya started to lift the third magic pencil wand into the air. "Should I use it now?"

"Hang on," gasped Jaden. "Wait till I get down. I don't want to have a bad accident."

As soon as he jumped Chaaya waved the wand, the object disappeared and the wand vanished too, but what was now filling up the yard took their breath away. The first object had contained their typical weekly shopping and the second one thirty sets of it, but today's looked like there must be twice as many as the last one. There were also four more lovely baskets full of fruit and vegetables. Chaaya was correct when she declared, "All that stuff takes up more space than the thing it came in!"

As they ate their breakfast the three of them talked about what to do with the incredible amount of food in their back yard. Because they had taken the second delivery to the houses in their street they wondered if they should deliver the food to some different homes this time but, as Chaaya said, "Whoever we give the food to, someone who really needs it could miss out and that wouldn't be fair."

Realising that she would soon have to set off to work, Dayana made a quick decision. She knew there must be some way of identifying the neediest in the town and that someone might know who and where they were. She asked Jaden to see if Shahid would use his laptop to find out if anyone could collect the food and distribute it to the people who needed it most. "Yes, but Mum, if we tell Shahid about it he'll be just as shocked as we are by what's happening. We can't expect him to believe that it all just appeared by magic!"

"Shahid is a good man. Tell him the truth and ask him to respect our wish to tell no-one else what has been happening to us. We've already said that that nobody would believe us if we told the true story, and I'm sure Shahid will realise that too."

"In any case," added Chaaya, "We only know a little bit of the truth, and if any of us, including Shahid, were to tell people what happened without explaining it all, they would make fun of us and accuse us of telling lies or being crazy people!"

When Dayana had reluctantly left for work, Jaden knocked on Shahid's door. He had never invited himself into Shahid's house, but today he asked if they could both sit down because there was something important to discuss.

Ten minutes later Shahid had heard the full story. As Chaaya predicted, at first, he thought Jaden was telling him a fairy story. But there was such seriousness in the boy's tone of voice that told him something out of the ordinary had taken place.

"So, you want me to use the laptop to search for organisations that can distribute food to the needy?"

"Yes. Do you think there will be any people like that round here?"

"I know there's a food bank somewhere in town because there's a collection point at the supermarket. I'll see what I can find." Remembering that Chaaya must be left on her own he asked, "Should I come to your house to do it?"

"That's a good idea, yeah, but there's something else I need to tell you first." Jaden was thinking about what Carl had told him, that there were lots of rough sleepers worse off even than him in Paradise Street. Surely, they would be some of the neediest? Now that Shahid knew about the weekly groceries, Jaden could also tell him about taking snacks to a man who slept in cardboard boxes, and the man asking him if he wanted to meet the other rough sleepers who would need support if any were available. Jaden also admitted to being wary about meeting up with the rough sleepers and would only agree to it if an adult could go with him.

There was such a lot for Shahid to take in. He didn't understand a lot of what Jaden said and realised that before he could properly assess the situation, he would need to see the scale of the mysterious delivery for himself. Picking up his laptop, he followed Jaden to number 24, and they walked through the house and out of the back door to face the reality he had first thought to be a fairy story.

16. The Busiest Day of All: Part One

Jaden hadn't told Chaaya about first meeting Sally in the back yard of number 2 Paradise Street but now he was going to have to explain that finding her had led him to also meet a man called Carl. He chose to tell her the full story in front of Shahid so that he too could understand that some of the food should be taken to the people in that street. At first, Chaaya was upset that Jaden hadn't told her sooner, but Shahid explained that what Jaden had done was brave and extremely kind and she started to understand. Shahid also told Jaden that he would now need to tell his mum the full story too, and Chaaya agreed to support him when the time came.

Shahid suggested that he should meet Carl if possible, and he would find out more about how many people in Paradise Street they might be able to help by giving them some of the food. He asked Jaden if he would take him to where Carl might be found, so that he could try talking to Carl while Jaden came straight back home to be with Chaaya. For her part, Chaaya could start using the laptop to find out about the food bank and see if there might be any other schemes in the town that could help distribute food as soon as possible.

On their short walk to the alleyway leading to Paradise Street's back yards, Shahid and Jaden discussed the best way to approach Carl and the other people who lived there. Jaden had brought a chocolate orange, a bunch of bananas, two packets of crisps, six apples, a loaf of bread, two packets of cheese, a jar of jam, two packets of biscuits, and a bottle of orange juice to give to Carl. He hoped that Carl would understand that, if he wanted all the rough sleepers to receive a set like his, he would need to meet Shahid first.

There was one more thing Shahid needed to know. Jaden lowered his voice as they approached the alleyway, and he quietly said, "Please don't be too surprised if Carl calls me Usain."

"Why would he do that?"

"Because I told him that's my name. I thought it would be best if he didn't know my real name because I was scared to tell him it when I met him."

"That was probably a good idea, really. Yes, I'll go along with that."

"Thanks. Right, this is it; you wait until I've had a quick look to see if he's there. I'll let you know if he agrees to meet you."

"Okay. You won't hear a squeak from me."

Jaden slipped quietly into the back yard of number 2. Carl was sitting up, surrounded by his boxes. "Hello? Oh, it's you, Usain. Come on in, kiddo." Carl sounded to be in a brighter mood than the last time Jaden saw him.

"Hi Carl." Jaden opened his bag and removed the contents, putting them all down on a bit of old newspaper. He decided to explain the reason for his visit without further delay. "My family has a lot of packs of food like this one, which is for you. And I..."

Carl interrupted before Jaden could continue. "That's really kind, Usain, and I'll enjoy an apple, but

I would like to share the rest of it with the others I told you about."

"This is all for you, and there are lots of sets just like it, so all the people you know in the street can have a full pack too."

Carl could hardly believe what he had just heard. "Are you serious?"

"Yes! You remember I told you I have a friend who's a student? He will need to help us because there's a lot of food to carry."

Carl hesitated, then, still uncertain, decided to cautiously go along with what Jaden was saying. "Okay, I see what you mean. But can I meet your student friend first?"

Seizing his chance, Jaden took a couple of steps back towards where Shahid was waiting and hissed, "Come on in - it's fine!" Then, turning back to Carl, he said, "This is Shahid."

Shahid approached Carl and held out his hand. "I'm pleased to meet you, sir." Carl slowly stretched out his right hand and the two men both smiled.

Jaden then explained, "I have to go back to be with my little sister now, Carl, because she's on her own in our house. Shahid will talk to you about when we can bring the food for everybody." He turned and left before Carl had a chance to object.

Shahid started to talk about the promised delivery to all in Paradise Street, and Carl soon became fully cooperative, realising that here was a genuine chance to provide at least a little of what was needed to give everyone a full stomach for once. He took Shahid along the back street, stopping every now and then to show him where people spent most of their time. As they walked, Shahid made a mental note of how many sets of food would be needed. He saw some of the people and a few spoke briefly to him, but most were covered by blankets, coats, boxes, or anything else they had found to use for shelter and warmth, and those people remained silent. Eventually the two men reached the end of the street and calculated that there were around twenty people to feed that day.

They returned to the back yard of number 2 and sat down together.

"When would be the best time to bring the food round?" asked Shahid.

"Could we say late afternoon?"

"I don't see why not. We'll have everything sorted out by then."

Carl changed the subject. "So how do you know Usain?"

"He lives near me, and I sometimes look after him and his sister. They're good kids."

"Usain seems to be a grand lad. His family must be proud of him."

"I'm sure that's true." Shahid didn't feel he should go into any further detail.

"I have a son who must be around Usain's age," revealed Carl, "But I haven't seen him or his mother for about ten years. I wish I could, but they wouldn't want to see me after what I did."

Feeling awkward that he had heard something that perhaps he had no right to know, but also interested in Carl's obviously difficult life, Shahid asked, "Go on, why haven't you seen them?"

Carl took a deep breath as if he were about to confess to a crime. He looked straight into Shahid's trusting brown eyes. "When my boy was a baby, I was doing terrible things, bad stuff, and I got real confused and started to hate myself. I was bad for my wife and was worried that I might do something stupid to ruin their lives as well as mine. I knew I had to get help and I left them. I ended up in London. There were other people there like me and I stayed for a couple of years. Things got worse; I lost more than half my body weight. Sometimes I thought I would die." He stopped and took another deep breath.

"I'm really sorry to hear that, Carl." Shahid tried to say something positive. "But you're here now and I guess you are a lot better."

"I am in some ways. Some good people who I call angels found me and took me to a centre for homeless people. Then they got me into a special clinic, all paid for by some rich guy, and I changed. It took years, but I changed."

"You must be so grateful to those people who helped you."

"Oh yeah, but I was the one who wanted to change, and some don't have that choice. Anyway, I wanted to come back to where I used to belong, and I've been here for a couple of months now."

"Is this how your life is going to be from now on?"

"Oh, I don't know. I want things to get better, but I don't know how to take the next step. It just feels like it would be impossible. I might just move on, maybe try Scotland."

Shahid was beginning to feel totally useless. He understood a little about Carl's life now, but only just as much as Carl wanted him to know. He had also just seen other people who, as Carl had said, were much worse off than him, and he assumed that they would all have back stories if they chose to tell them. Maybe they would need to find a more positive state of mind and body, like Carl, before they could say anything to anyone else. He thought it was time to get back to the children and stood up, but Carl wanted to say something else. Shahid could see that tears had formed in his eyes and his cheeks were wet. "I know I'm not far from my wife and my Jaden, but I don't know what to do about it."

Shahid could not have expected to hear those few words, and he was suddenly shocked. "What did you say your son's name was?"

Carl took a deep breath. "We called him Jaden. It means 'God has heard'. I wonder if he knows that."

Shahid thought he should leave and collect his own thoughts, but he needed to check one more thing before he could be sure of his facts. "It's been great meeting you, Carl."

"Good to see you too. I'll see you again this afternoon."

"I'm looking forward to it!" He held out his hand once again. "By the way, my full name is Shahid Nanda."

Carl's smiling response told him all he needed to know. "I'm Carlton Williams, my friend."

17. The Busiest Day of All: Part Two

Shahid's mind was racing as he walked back to Rankin Street. Not only had he seen the incredible and baffling food delivery for himself, but he had also met many rough sleepers living close to his own home, and he had just become the only person who knew that Dayana's husband was just round the corner, desperate to finally get his life sorted out. Poor Carlton Williams didn't realise that he had met his own son, or that he had a daughter. Shahid was aware that that he must be careful not to tell the children anything at the moment, but surely, he was going to have to share what he knew with Dayana, and that would have to be carefully and sensitively handled.

During the short time when Jaden was out with Shahid, Chaaya used the laptop to find information about the nearest food bank. She read all about the wonderful work done by those who give their time to put donated food into special boxes that provide a few days' worth of nutritionally balanced meals for individuals and families. As soon as Jaden came back, she told him all about it. "I'm sure we could give most of our stuff to the food bank because they need the things that we are ready to give."

"What sort of food do they want?" asked Jaden.

Chaaya read out the list she had found. "Soup, pasta, rice, tinned tomatoes, lentils, pasta sauce, beans and pulses, tinned meat, tinned fish, fresh bread, tinned vegetables, tea and coffee, tinned fruit, biscuits, UHT milk and fruit juice, but they will take some other things too."

She repeated the news when Shahid re-joined them. He thought the food bank would be pleased to hear from them, and added, "We might need to see if anyone else is operating a similar service too. And I've just found out that we need to get twenty sets of food ready for Paradise Street later this afternoon." Jaden and Shahid winked and gave each other a thumbs-up.

Another session searching the internet for other local initiatives led to an exciting discovery. The town now had something called an Interfaith Group, and it supported a team of volunteers who would collect food from those offering donations and take it to a church hall where they could sort it all, ready to be given directly into the hands of those people in the town who couldn't afford to buy food. The team had only been set up a few weeks ago and, as Shahid said, now would be a good time to support them too.

"It looks as if we have a lot to do," said Jaden. "We need to plan who does what."

"Right then," Chaaya said decisively. She was feeling like being organiser-in-chief. "How about Shahid phoning the food bank and the Interfaith Group to tell them what we have and ask if they can come to pick it up while Jaden and I sort out all the food into different types that will be suitable for each of the groups?"

"That's a great plan!" added Shahid. "Then I can join you with the sorting. We will need to put the items for the different groups into different places, so we could have the food for Paradise Street in twenty packs in the back yard, everything for the food bank in the front room and the food for the Interfaith Group in the kitchen."

"That's it all decided then," concluded Jaden. "Let's do it!"

Three hours of planning, sorting, organising, and communicating followed. Shahid heard the surprise and delight of volunteers at both the food bank and the Interfaith Group. He explained that, as some of the food was fresh, it was important that it reached those who needed it as soon as possible. With the food bank van due to arrive at 2.30 pm and Interfaith Group members in their own cars following shortly after that, Chaaya and Jaden needed to work quickly. Eventually, at around 2.10 pm everything was in place. Jaden waited at the end of the street to direct the van towards the narrow entrance to the back yards, Chaaya put the food for the Interfaith Group in rows leading to the front door and Shahid checked the bags that would be taken to Paradise Street.

The food bank van was on time. It was too wide to be driven into the alleyway, so Chaaya, Jaden and Shahid had to carry all the food from the back of number 24. They then helped Theresa, the delighted driver, to load it up. "The van's not been as full as this before," she exclaimed, laughing. When the last items had been loaded and the van doors closed she asked, "So where did all this stuff come from?"

Chaaya had anticipated being asked this and replied, "Let's just say it's from someone who is really kind and generous," and she saw the others nodding approval at her answer.

"Well, whoever they are, please pass on our grateful thanks," said Theresa.

Just as Theresa was leaving there was a knock at the front door and Pastor Joseph of the Interfaith Group introduced himself to Chaaya. Looking at all the food lined up in the front room, he asked, "How much of this is for us to take?"

Chaaya grinned. "All of it."

Pastor Joseph took out his phone. "I think I'd better warn the others that we will need to make a few journeys. We could only find five people with cars this afternoon."

It was almost 4.15 pm when the final car left with the food that had been donated to the Interfaith Group. Some of the drivers had to make four journeys to take everything to the parish hall.

Shahid was just about to remind Chaaya and Jaden that it was time to go to Paradise Street with the final set of deliveries when Pastor Joseph unexpectedly returned.

"I just wanted to let you all know that we are incredibly grateful for your donations. They will be distributed today and tomorrow."

"We're so pleased that we could help," said Shahid, "But we're sorry that we won't be able to give this amount of food again. This was a one-off."

"I totally understand. We only recently started the food parcel distribution, and this will show people that we are serious about making a real difference to some of the neediest members of the town."

Shahid asked who the Interfaith Group members were, and Joseph explained that all the town's religious groups had come together to decide how they could usefully support the community. Shahid was keen to find out more and, without hesitation, he asked, "Is there a chance that I could join the group? Today has made me realise that our one day of donations should only be the beginning of something that continues and grows."

Joseph put a hand onto Shahid's shoulder and smiled warmly. "Yes please. You would be most welcome. Your experience today will, I hope, inspire others to donate too. And we can never have too many volunteers."

Chaaya wanted to say something. "What about me? Can I join too?"

"And don't forget me," added Jaden.

The pastor looked at the siblings and saw the honesty and kindness in their faces. "We haven't really thought about children helping," he said openly, "But you two would be wonderful members."

Shahid intervened. "Perhaps they could come with me? I would promise to look after them and I know they would be a great help." Pastor Joseph explained that he would have to talk to the other group leaders about allowing children to take part, but he was in no doubt that something good could come out of their participation.

"It has been a great pleasure to meet you all, and now I must go back to the others; they'll think I'm leaving them to do all the work."

Shahid added, "I'll be in touch soon." He decided not to tell the pastor about the Paradise Street community just yet. He wanted to see how today's delivery would work out first, but he had every intention to find a way of continuing what was just beginning there.

Fifteen minutes later, twenty bags of food for the rough sleepers had been brought through to the front room. Shahid asked Chaaya to stay at home, knowing that Dayana would soon be back from work.

Jaden helped Shahid to carry the bags to the end of the alleyway leading to Paradise Street. It took the two of them four journeys to take everything carefully to and from Jaden's house. Finally, Shahid asked Jaden to go back to Chaaya; he didn't want

Jaden to become too involved with the rough sleepers and was also concerned that Carl might want to say more about his 'lost' family. Shahid knew that he had a lot of serious thinking to do!

18. The Busiest Day of All: Part Three

Dayana arrived home just after Jaden. She looked around the house and the back yard and saw that all the packs of weekly groceries had gone. Chaaya was watching a very happy and healthy guinea pig running round and round the settee and Jaden was lying on the floor, exhausted but hoping that Claude might run to him and stop for a stroke. Dayana assumed that the question she was about to ask would lead to a long discussion. "So, have you had a busy day?"

After telling their mother the story of the day's incredible events the children remembered that they hadn't eaten anything since early morning. Their work had taken such concentrated effort that, even though being surrounded by food, it somehow hadn't occurred to them to eat. Satisfying meals for three humans and one guinea pig were greatly enjoyed that evening.

Shahid's experience in Paradise Street was mostly successful. Carl helped him to carry the bags to the rough sleepers, standing back while Shahid left them next to each person there, saying, "This is for you." Some of the people spoke, and others said nothing. A few stayed underneath the boxes, blankets, or other covers, and Shahid hoped they would find the food after he had gone.

When the final bag had been left with Carl, Shahid felt a great sense of satisfaction but was also acutely aware that people were receiving an abundance of food today but nothing tomorrow. He resolved to tell Pastor Joseph about the Paradise Street community, hoping that support might continue in some way.

As Shahid was about to leave and return to Rankin Street, Carl suddenly said, "That was a good thing to do, my friend, and it's got me thinking. I'm ready."

"Ready for what?"

"Ready to move on. I'm going to see if Scotland is ready for me."

Shahid stopped in his tracks. "Why do you want to go there?"

"To start all over again. When I'm here I just get upset, thinking about what I had and what I lost. If I go a long way away, I might be able to clear out my head and maybe get a job. And I'll also try to do what you did today; I can help rough sleepers because I understand them."

Shahid couldn't say what he was thinking, but he said, "Before you decide to leave, will you do something for me?"

"What on earth could I do for you?"

"Will you stay a few more days at least and help me to put together a plan for finding ways to help support the people living in Paradise Street? I know someone who can help us; his name is Joseph. And if you do that it will help you to prepare for what you want to do when you meet the rough sleepers in Scotland."

Carl considered this offer carefully. "I suppose it could be useful," he said eventually. "Maybe I'll give it another week."

Shahid wasn't sure why he had mentioned Pastor Joseph. Of course, his main concern was to share his new-found information about Carl with Dayana. Finding out not only that her husband was alive but also that he was living close by was going to come as a shock to her, and Shahid couldn't predict how she would respond. Dayana would have to then decide what, if anything, to do and how or how not to involve the children. As of right now, Shahid was well aware that he was the only person who knew that Carl had already met his son and that he was not aware that he had a daughter. Shahid was carrying a burden of responsibility that was almost too much for him to bear.

19. The Birth of Midnight Grocers

Amber was about to try the back door of her neighbour's house on Sunday morning when she heard an unfamiliar squeaking sound. Looking to where it was coming from, she saw the hutch and then Claude. She reacted in the same way as most people do when they see a guinea pig looking at them. "Oh, you are lovely. What's your name?"

The back door opened. "My name's Chaaya, of course, and he is Claude."

The two girls hugged each other. "It was a great holiday but it's good to come home." Amber wondered why Chaaya was still wearing pyjamas as she was usually dressed much earlier in the morning.

"I was tired, so I had a lie in." Chaaya had no intention of telling Amber about the previous day's events. She and Jaden had decided that it was going to be less hassle just to keep it to themselves, at least for the time being.

"Your guinea pig is lovely. Can I hold him?"

"Claude's not mine. He belongs to Sally."

"Who?"

"You know, that girl we met in the park before you went on holiday. She's really nice." One thing she was happy to share with Amber was the story of Claude's illness, the visit to the vet and how she had become friends with Sally.

No sooner had Chaaya finished telling Amber the story than Sally had joined them in the back yard. "Are you talking about me?" she asked cheerfully, then, "Hello, Amber. It's good to see you again."

Amber thought it strange that Sally spoke as if they knew each other well, but appreciated the friendliness in her voice. "Claude is lovely, isn't he? Please can I hold him?"

Sally opened the hutch door and could see such a huge difference in Claude's health. "You're looking and sounding like your old self again, little chap. I'm sure you'd like to meet Amber."

A few moments later the three girls were playing with Claude in the front room. The door from the bottom of the stairs opened and a yawning Jaden, also still in his pyjamas, muttered in a sleepy voice, "What's all this noise about?"

Amber was surprised at Jaden's late arrival too. He was usually out and about with his friends by this time, and she said, "Not another sleepy head? What on earth were you two doing yesterday?"

By 10.00 am Amber had told her friends all about her holiday. Chaaya was pleased to hear everything Amber shared with them; she occasionally felt disappointed that her own family couldn't afford to go away for breaks, but this time she had no doubt that her experiences while Amber was away had been far more exciting than a holiday.

Shahid called on the hour as usual and spoke to Jaden. He revealed that he had overslept too but was now wide awake and wondered if they would all like to join him for a kickabout football session. Jaden asked the others, and they were all keen to get out together, so he and Chaaya quickly dressed while Amber and Sally spent more precious time with Claude.

The kickabout was enjoyed by all. As before, they took it in turns to be goalkeeper while the others played passing and shooting. By now, Jaden could clearly tell that his sister and her friends loved playing football almost as much as him. After a good hour, with all five feeling in need of a rest, they sat beneath a tree, chatting and laughing until Sally, suddenly looking more serious, said, "There's something I have to tell you all." The others stopped what they were doing and looked at her, feeling that an announcement might follow. "I have loved visiting you very much." She paused, struggling with her feelings, "But I have to go home tomorrow, back to my family."

After an awkward silence, Chaaya asked, "Will you come back to see us again?"

"I don't know. I want to, of course, and I'm going to ask the grown-ups if I can come again next summer." Of course, the Earth humans wouldn't be able to begin to comprehend what Sally would have to do to return, but she had formulated a plan. It would involve a follow-up mission the following summer, the reason for it being to update her current work by evaluating the progress made by the family in their aim to work as volunteers with the Interfaith Group. Sally felt that, because this year's mission was going to report on important beginnings, a follow-up would be justifiable, and it would be something that Professor Xander would undoubtedly support.

"I have an important announcement to make too," said Jaden. "Tomorrow there's going to be another football tournament in the park."

Chaaya thought she knew what Jaden was going to say next and quickly said, "Yes, okay. We'll come to watch you. Just don't get injured this time."

Jaden smiled. "No, I wasn't going to ask you that." He went on to ask something that surprised and delighted them all. "This time a lot of the usual crowd are away on their holidays and Big Harry has organised it as a four-a-side tournament. I would like you three girls to be in my team."

Chaaya felt herself glowing with pride in her brother for accepting her and the other girls as footballers. The three of them shouted, "Yes, yes,

yes," and all four members of the new team stood up, instantly joining hands in a circle, and throwing them in the air together. Shahid was delighted too, and he felt so proud of them all.

When they had all calmed down a little Chaaya said, "I have an idea for our team's name - Midnight Grocers!"

"That's perfect!" agreed Jaden, knowing that the name meant something special to Chaaya and himself, and that the others wouldn't mind even if they didn't know why it had been chosen. However, Sally had a little chuckle to herself, knowing that she was the true midnight grocer!

Shahid texted Dayana as soon as he got home. His message said, "Everything is fine here. The children have had a great day. Please could you call to see me on your way home?" He had been wondering how to tell her about Carl and wanted to get it right. The best way to proceed, he told himself, was to tell Dayana the truth. The news would come as a massive shock at first, and he knew it would eventually be up to her to do whatever she felt to be best for everyone concerned.

Back at number 24, Jaden was talking tactics to his team. "Big Harry says we'll all play four matches, so we'll take it in turns to be goalie. I'll go in goal for the first match. Amber, you stay back in defence and concentrate on clearing the ball away as far as you can. Sally, you play up and down the pitch on the right and Chaaya, you do the same on the left. When Sally gets the ball Chaaya runs forward and gets ready to go for goal, and Chaaya does the same when Sally gets the ball. When you have the ball at your feet and can see their goal, shoot with all your power. When one of you is our goalie, I'll fill in your position. Have you all got that?"

The other three looked happily at Jaden and each of them said, "Got it," in unison. Each one had a picture in their mind of what was expected of them. The excitement in the room was intense, and Chaaya told Jaden he would be a Premier League manager one day.

When all had been decided Sally said, "I'd better be getting back to where I'm staying now and I'm sorry to say that Claude will have to come with me this time."

"Can we have one last cuddle with him?" asked Chaaya.

"Of course you can," Sally replied. "You are the ones who saved his life, and he loves you like I do."

"You sloppy lump!" said Jaden, and Midnight Grocers giggled happily together.

Chaaya and Jaden thought their mum must be working late that night. Of course, they had no idea that she had called to see Shahid. When Dayana eventually came through the door she went straight past the children to the bathroom. They hadn't noticed that she had been crying, and after washing her face she came downstairs and immediately threw her arms round them, saying, "I love you both so much. You know that don't you?"

"Yes Mum," replied Jaden, "But what's for tea?"

20. The End of the Mission

It was going to be difficult for Sally to leave her Earth friends, but she felt confident that she would have a good reason to return, hopefully next year. However, she was also missing her own family a lot and was looking forward to being back home on Planet 3. In addition, Claude shouldn't be spending too long in the personal caravan, which clearly wasn't providing the best environment for a guinea pig. Professor Xander would need to ask the scientists who created it to improve the Eco-tech and the fresh air and water systems if pets were to accompany their owners on future missions.

But today was the final day of the mission, and one thing dominated Sally's thoughts: she had been asked to play in a football tournament and she was going to enjoy it!

Headband in place, Sally arrived at the park just before the rest of her teammates. A lot of other boys were already there, and Sally had seen some of them before. One was Baz, who also recognised her. He called out, "I see the posh girl has come to watch us win." Sally ignored him and sat on the swing, looking in the opposite direction. Jaden, Chaaya and Amber, all wearing white t-shirts, saw that Sally was looking a bit anxious and ran towards her. Jaden was carrying a white t-shirt for Sally, and she put in on over her own blue top.

"Now we look like a team," declared Jaden.

Baz noticed that Jaden and the girls were now dressed in the same-coloured shirts. "Hey, Williams, don't tell me this is your team," he bellowed, drawing everyone's attention to what he was announcing.

Jaden stared at him and said, "You look surprised to see us, Baz. I hope you won't be surprised when we beat your lot."

Chaaya wished Jaden had kept quiet, and now she was feeling under pressure. She gathered the team round her. "Do you really think we can win?"

Jaden, also wishing he hadn't replied to Baz, said, "We might lose every game, but let's just enjoy playing. The results don't matter." Chaaya felt proud of her brother; she had thought of him as having 'must score' and 'must win' attitudes, but now he suddenly seemed to have changed. Could it be that the way he had responded to the needy people, giving them time and food, had helped him to get his priorities right?

After a sleepless night Dayana decided that, for the first time ever, she would request a morning off work without pay "for personal reasons." Her manager agreed, knowing full well that she must have a good reason for asking because Dayana was a reliable, hard worker who needed whatever pay she could get. She left the house at the usual time and, conscious that the children had no idea what she was up to, walked the short distance to number 28 where Shahid was waiting to talk to her once again.

Midnight Grocers' first match started very badly. Straight from the kick-off Jaden's friend Kim, who was captaining Kim's Kickers, dribbled round Sally and Amber before scoring past goalkeeper Jaden. However, from that moment on Jaden was unbeatable in goal; he played like a professional (or so he said later) and kept the score down to a respectable 1-0 with save after save thwarting the Kickers' many chances.

In their second match, against Tearaways, the Grocers played well, with Jaden dominating possession both in attack and by working like two people (or so he said later) to keep the ball well away from Sally's goal. Amber and Chaaya were really beginning to understand what was needed to link up with their team members. In typical Jaden style, he ran towards the Tearaways' goal at pace with the ball seemingly attached to his feet and chipping it over the advancing goalkeeper, scored a great goal. Unfortunately, Sally couldn't quite manage to reach a good shot which, with the last kick of the game, meant the result was a 1-1 draw.

Chaaya went in goal for the third match, against City United, and Midnight Grocers struggled to find a way through a resolute defence, although Jaden hit a powerful shot against a post in the second half. He also managed to throw himself in front of a goal-bound attempt that would have otherwise hit a spectator behind the goal and broken his nose (or so he said later). The result was a second draw for the Grocers, this time 0-0.

The fourth and final match was to be played against Baz's team, Bazzaboys, who had won two matches and drawn one to this point. Before the match started, Jaden called his team to him. "We've played really well so far," he said, encouragingly.

"We haven't won though," added Amber.

"That doesn't matter. You have all showed the rest of them just how good you are. I'm really glad I picked you for my team. Now we're going to have the hardest match of all. If Bazzaboys beat us they'll have won the tournament, so let's give it everything!"

The girls agreed to work even harder than in the other matches, but Sally was looking rather anxious. "Is everything alright?" asked Chaaya.

"Yes, apart from one thing: it's getting a bit late for me really. I have to go home soon, in about ten minutes, and I need to check on Claude before we go just to make sure he's still happy and well. Sorry, but

I'll go straight after the final whistle." The others understood and they gave Sally a team hug. She added, "I won't hang around at the end, but you know I'll never forget you all."

Sally's words made the others feel sad, but they also seemed to give them even greater determination to play their hearts out for one last time. As the teams lined up Baz, always the confident one, screamed, "Let's get 'em!" and the match began at a frantic pace. Amber was on great form in goal, leaping at the ball every time it came near her. Time after time she seemed to have the amazing ability to get in the way of every one of Baz's shots. Early in the second half, Amber kicked the ball up to the halfway line, where Jaden jumped and headed it over Baz towards the Bazzaboys' goal. Sally quickly spotted where the ball was going, and she sprinted forward before kicking it over the line with the keeper well beaten. Jaden's header was probably the greatest flick-on ever seen in the history of the world (or so he said later). Baz turned to Sally and muttered, "Good goal. I don't know how you could even see that ball coming when Jaden flicked it on."

"It's not that difficult if you have eyes in the back of your head," said Sally.

In the final few minutes Bazzaboys, desperate for the win, threw everything at Midnight Grocers. With just a few seconds left to play Baz took a corner that was heading straight into the goalmouth. Amber leapt into the air and punched the ball away. Just three or so meters from her own goal, Chaaya saw the ball land in front of her, her right leg swung back, then forward, and the ball flew the full length of the pitch straight into the opposition goal with the most wonderful *'WHOOSH'* she had ever heard. Her ultimate golden sound had come at the best possible time. After their 2-0 defeat, Baz and his teammates shook hands with each of Midnight Grocers and then Big Harry led three cheers for Kim's Kickers, who had won the tournament.

Chaaya, Jaden and Amber got together for a final team huddle. Sally was nowhere to be seen. "She didn't say goodbye," said Amber, disappointedly.

"It's very hard to say goodbye sometimes," Jaden explained.

Chaaya ran towards the park entrance and, with no-one else near her, she shouted, "Sally - please come back one day!"

No voice replied but Chaaya could hear a distant sound. She knew exactly what it was. It was the unmistakeable '*WHOOOOOOSH*' of the midnight grocer.

Afterwords - extracts from the diaries of Chaaya and Jaden Williams

Jaden, Wednesday 11 August

Carl is my dad!!!!!!!!!!! His full name is Carlton Williams. He has been sleeping on Shahid's settee for the last two nights. Shahid told Mum that he found out about him, and Mum has met him twice. I hope he isn't upset with me for saying my name was Usain.

Chaaya, Wednesday 11 August

Mum just told me that my dad has come to Shahid's house. We are going to see him soon. I hope he is a nice man. I feel very strange inside.

Jaden, Thursday 12 August

We went to see our dad at Shahid's house. He looks all clean and tidy now and he smiles a lot. We all cried – Shahid too. Dad didn't talk much but I think he will when I tell him about football.

Chaaya, Thursday 12 August

My dad told me I have a lovely name and then we started crying. He is very handsome and was wearing Shahid's suit. I think he looks like me, and Shahid and Mum agree. I want him to be happy.

Chaaya, Sunday 22 August

Tonight, my dad came to our house. He said he liked the carpets and the colours of the walls.

Jaden, Saturday 28 August

Last night I told Dad about football, and he said he likes it too, so we're going to play with him one day. He also told me that he snores a lot!

Jaden, Sunday 29 August

We all went with Shahid to the Interfaith Group, and we helped to put food into parcels. Shahid and Dad are going to start taking parcels to Paradise Street and Pastor Joseph said Dad is a walking miracle.

Chaaya, Saturday 13 September

Dad has got a real job! Mrs Fred at Fred's Friendly Fryer is retiring, and Dad is taking over as assistant fryer. Mum and Dad are both very happy about it and so am I.

Jaden, Monday 15 September

Something incredible and wonderful happened today. Dad wanted to celebrate his first day at work. He asked Chaaya and me to close our eyes and when we opened them, we saw he was holding a rabbit!!!!!!! He said it was for us and I just feel great. The rabbit is so snuggly.

<u>Chaaya, Saturday 13 September</u>

We now have a lovely grey rabbit with a white stripe from the top of her head to the tip of her nose. Dad brought her for us. She has gone to live in the palace where Claude stayed when he was ill. We have named her Claudette. I feel as if all my wishes have come true and I love all my family, Mum, Dad, and Jaden.

MISSION REPORT

Name: Sally Kwolek **Age:** 10 years 10 months

Teacher: Professor Xander

Purpose of Mission: To assess whether or not the selected family and their contacts are capable of selfless acts that improve the wellbeing of others.

Timescale: 18 days, Friday 23 July – Monday 9 August

Funding received: 10,500 sperglons

DATE	SIGNIFICANT EVENT	NAMES OF THOSE INVOLVED	HOW EVIDENCED	RELEVANT BEHAVIOUR	NOTES
Friday 23 July	First day of mission				
Friday 23 July	Sibling conversation. CW wanted to be able to join in with football game	Chaaya Williams (CW), Jaden Williams (JW)	Orconiwave viewer	JW found excuse to forbid it. JW selfish/embarrassed?	Further investigation necessary
Friday 23 July	1st silvercrate delivered to 24 Rankin Street at midnight				

Saturday 24 July	Silvercrate discovered	Chaaya Williams, Amber Hodgson (AH) (neighbour)	Orconiwave viewer	CW & AH reacted with surprise and shock	I felt excited!
Saturday 24 July	1 Observed football (boys only) at park 2 First meeting with Earth humans at park	1 Jaden Williams, other boys 2 Chaaya Williams, Amber Hodgson	Observation and direct contact	Boys played football. Girls watched. Selfish behaviour by boys? Boys' attitude accepted by girls?	Discrimination on grounds of gender?
Saturday 24 July	Football at park When JW was injured, CW kicked ball very hard	Jaden Williams, other boys, Chaaya Williams, Amber Hodgson	Orconiwave viewer	JW embarrassed and AH shocked by CW's behaviour	It appeared that it was not acceptable for a girl to join in with the game of football. Gender issue confirmed
Saturday 24 July	DW shown silvercrate, weekly shopping revealed	Chaaya Williams, Mrs Dayana Williams (DW)	Orconiwave viewer	Mrs DW was also surprised and shocked. Grateful to accept food as gift	
Saturday 24 July	Acted part of crying child at 2 Paradise Street in order to attract attention of passing boys and see what their response would be	Jaden Williams	Direct contact	JW came to help and showed concern. Caring response. Went home and returned with food despite being injured. Selfless and kind despite his own fears	Three other boys left JW to investigate and they went home. All had been instructed by their parents not to go into Paradise Street
Saturday 24 July	Met CH & AH at park – brief conversation. Saw JW playing football with other boys	Chaaya Williams, Amber Hodgson	Direct contact	CW & AH friendly. JW saw me but avoided me. Embarrassed to be seen talking to a girl?	CW told me that her teacher has eyes in the back of her head

Saturday 24 July	Went to house of teacher who I suspected was visiting from Planet 3	Miss Robinson (Miss R) (teacher)	Direct contact	Despite not knowing me, Miss R showed a lot of kindness and concern, suspecting that I was in some kind of danger	Believing that Miss R was a Planet 3 human, I removed my wig. She fainted but recovered. Serious error of judgement which I regret
Friday 30 July	Evening meal at neighbour's house. Neighbours explained they were about to go on holiday	Chaaya Williams, Jaden Williams, Mrs Dayana Williams, Amber Hodgson, Mrs L Hodgson, Mr J Hodgson	Orconiwave viewer	Hodgson family were careful to show empathy for Williams family who could not afford a holiday	
Friday 30 July	2nd silvercrate delivered to 24 Rankin Street at midnight				
Saturday 31 July	2nd silvercrate discovered	Chaaya Williams, Jaden Williams	Orconiwave viewer	1 CW & JW uncertain what to do with food 2 JW initially surprised and shocked, then remembered meeting me as someone in need, and his care for my situation caused him to react with kindness	1 Decided to wait until Mrs DW returned 2 JW did not tell CW about me but left home with food for me

Saturday 31 July	JW took food to 2 Paradise Street. He expected to see me but met Carl and gave him food	JW, Carl (homeless man)	Orconiwave viewer	JW understood how good it feels to give to those in need. He showed increasing kindness to others	JW showed kindness and told nobody else about what he had done. Selfless behaviour
Saturday 31 July	SN began to call in order to see if CW and JW were safe and well every hour during day	Mr Shahid Nanda (SN) (neighbour)	Orconiwave viewer	SN unselfishly gave up his time to look after neighbour's children	SN committed to caring for the children for the week
Saturday 31 July	JW asked SN if they could go out to play football and SN invited CW to join in	Chaaya Williams, Jaden Williams, Mr S Nanda	Orconiwave viewer	SN knew that girls can play football too which had an impact on JW and helped to include all in the activity	After playing football JW told Mrs DW that CW was 'brilliant', an important moment showing changing attitude
Saturday 31 July	After shock at sight of all food, DW informed CW and JW that the food must be shared with others	Chaaya Williams, Jaden Williams, Mrs D Williams	Orconiwave viewer	All three were immediately enthusiastic and showed understanding of the need to share. Totally unselfish	A significant observation of Earth humans' positive attitude to sharing
Saturday 31 July	CW, JW and DW delivered to every house in Rankin Street	Chaaya Williams, Jaden Williams, Mrs D Williams	Orconiwave viewer	All three exhibited much happiness after sharing	Doing things for others made these Earth humans feel good
Sunday 1 August	Residents of Rankin Street grateful for deliveries	Chaaya Williams, Jaden Williams, Mrs D Williams	Orconiwave viewer	Gratitude shown by majority of those receiving gifts	

Monday 2 August	Claude not well. Took him to 24 Rankin Street to seek help	Chaaya Williams, Jaden Williams, Mr S Nanda	Direct contact	CW, JW and SN very keen to help. Kind to Claude and me. SN led us to see vet	Doing things for others and animals made these Earth humans feel good
Monday 2 August	Visit to vet's surgery with Claude	Chaaya Williams, Jaden Williams, Mr S Nanda, Miss J Norman (JN) (vet), receptionist	Direct contact	Vet had a lovely manner and I trusted her. SN was prepared to pay entire fee – exceptional kindness. Vet intervened and said we didn't have to pay anything. Extremely kind	I felt confident that Claude would recover. SN and JN were generous with their money and time
Monday 2 August	Claude taken back to 24 Rankin Street	Chaaya Williams, Jaden Williams, Mrs D Williams, Mr S Nanda	Direct contact	DW provided rabbit hutch for Claude and offered to look after him. Offer gratefully accepted	Great kindness was shown to both Claude and me
Friday 6 August	JW made second visit to Carl with food	Jaden Williams, Carl	Orconiwave viewer (recorded)	Carl and JW both wanted to help others living rough in Paradise Street.	Carl recognised that others were worse off than him. He and JW shared desire to do something selfless
Friday 6 August	3rd silvercrate delivered to 24 Rankin Street at midnight				

Saturday 7 August	DW recognised the importance of identifying those most in need of food and asked CW & JW to involve SN in researching this	Chaaya Williams, Jaden Williams, Mrs D Williams, Mr S Nanda	Orconiwave viewer	DW showed kindness and compassion for those in need	DW had to go to work, so allocated roles to be carried out in her absence
Saturday 7 August	CW researched food bank and any other relevant groups while JW and SN visited Carl to find out about the needy in Paradise Street	Chaaya Williams, Jaden Williams, Mr S Nanda, Carl	Orconiwave viewer	All involved were now totally committed to making sure the food went to people who really needed it. Each person was taking responsibility. A great deal of selfless thought and action was taking place	Very significant selfless action took place
Saturday 7 August	Three groups to receive food identified by CW, JW & SN. (Paradise Street, Food Bank and Interfaith Group)	Chaaya Williams, Jaden Williams, Mr S Nanda	Orconiwave viewer	Three hours of planning, sorting, organising and communicating with relevant groups took place	
Saturday 7 August	Visited by representatives of Food Bank and Interfaith Group. Food collected by both organisations as organised by CW, JW & SN	Chaaya Williams, Jaden Williams, Mr S Nanda, Theresa (Food Bank), Pastor Joseph (Interfaith Group)	Orconiwave viewer	SN expressed wish to volunteer as member of Interfaith Group. CW & JW also wanted to be involved	Such a lot of good came from the way people responded to the 3rd silvercrate delivery. I saw very many examples of kindness, caring acts and selflessness

Saturday 7 August	SN and Carl distributed food to Paradise Street	Mr S Nanda, Carl	Orconiwave viewer	Carl told SN that he wanted to help the needy, possibly in Scotland. He was inspired to do so because of the food distribution, and it showed that he was in a positive state of mind	Carl's kindness despite his own situation was evidence of Earth humans' compassion for others
Sunday 8 August	JW asked CW, AH and me to be in his football team	Chaaya Williams, Jaden Williams, Amber Hodgson, Mr S Nanda	Direct contact	JW chose to have girls in his team. His attitude had been transformed	I felt nervous about playing in a tournament!
Monday 9 August	The football tournament took place. I played for Midnight Grocers	Chaaya Williams, Jaden Williams, Amber Hodgson	Direct contact	JW told us to enjoy playing, and that the results didn't matter. This showed that he wanted to involve the girls more than to win. His attitude was shown to be inclusive	I loved it!
Monday 9 August	The tournament ended. We didn't win every game but enjoyed playing well	Chaaya Williams, Jaden Williams, Amber Hodgson, other boys	Direct contact	Many handshakes and cheers from all (including Baz!) at the end of the tournament. Hopefully, this was a sign that, because JW showed that girls can play too, the inclusive attitude had begun to spread to others	I hope to return to Earth next year with a follow-up mission (see below)
Monday 9 August	End of mission				

Conclusions:

Many examples of selfishness, discrimination and anti-social behaviour have been observed on Earth. I wanted to find out, by observing and interacting with a small group of people, if Earth humans are capable of selfless acts that improve the wellbeing of others. I decided to send three silvercrates of food items to the back yard of 24 Rankin Street in order to discover if the family would keep everything for themselves, sell some of it to make money for themselves or share it with others.

Here are my findings:

- The first silvercrate, containing one week's shopping for the family, was kept for themselves. This outcome was expected because the family have very little money. However, human compassion for me (acting as a poor, hungry child) was observed when one child brought chocolate for me when he could have simply eaten it himself.
- When the second silvercrate was delivered, the same family member who had brought his chocolate to me immediately tried to find me in order to share again. He met a homeless man and gave it to him instead. The children relied upon their mother to decide what to do with all the food, and she said it should all be shared. They were both happy to agree with what she said, knowing that sharing was the right thing to do. They all felt much personal satisfaction at being able to do good by sharing the food.

- The arrival of the third silvercrate allowed the family to build upon the joy they felt when sharing with others, and contacting groups who could identify the needy was very important. Organising, planning, sorting and delivering was carried out with selfless enthusiasm. The contribution of an adult neighbour who shared their views was significant.
- Organisations such as food banks improve the lives of many. In addition, many faiths are able to work together with a common aim. Such organisations rely on volunteers to come forward. One example I observed was of the adult neighbour who recognised the good work being done by the Interfaith Group and wished to volunteer. The children who had worked with him asked if they could do the same. Strong leadership of voluntary groups was observed: this is crucial if such groups are to succeed.
- There are many homeless people and 'rough sleepers.' Some were identified, with the involvement of the homeless man being significant in this. He also wished to volunteer to help in some way. **There is goodness, kindness and selfless behaviour among Earth humans.**
- Something I did not expect to observe is how attitudes towards anti-discrimination and inclusion can be transformed: I saw the change from a 'no girls in football' attitude through to acceptance of their inclusion. This came about through a combination of factors: greater understanding of others by learning to share the food; family members working together; strong leadership from some boys and others (such as the neighbour); and understanding that it is right to include all others in whatever is taking place. This change shows that **positive change of attitudes can take place even where there has previously been a lack of care or compassion and selfishness.**

About the Author

As a father, teacher and headteacher, Brian Beresford has always enjoyed storytelling. He is also a composer and songwriter, producing music for schools in the UK and beyond. Whether writing stories or music for children, he aims to bring happiness to the reader, listener or performer. He hopes that 'The Midnight Grocer' is a book that the reader cannot bear to put down!

Cover illustration by Alexandra Kate Boswell

Acknowledgements

Brian wishes to thank Claire, Robert, Anna, Peter, Sara, John, Sue, Maria, Katie, Samira and Year 6 children at St Barnabas & St Paul's CE Primary School, Blackburn for their practical help and feedback.
Thanks also to Lionel Ross at i2i Publishing for his encouragement and support.

Please go to YouTube and find the song *'Midnight Grocer, Who are You? Chaaya's Song'*, which has been specially written and recorded for you to enjoy.

https://youtu.be/xL7glYY1olM

Follow the words and sing along!